Because It's Always You

Just Because, #4

Drew Duncan

For my Chris
You brought me back to life.
I am forever yours xx

Chapter One
Andy

Two years ago

Andrew Charles Reece.

I signed my name on the last copy and put the pen down. Just like that, it was done, and for the second time in my life, the man I loved let me down and was gone.

I wasn't even sure precisely where it all went wrong, I just know that, at the end, we had become two people with two very different ideas about where we wanted our lives to be going.

I wanted a family. I wanted to have the same things the average couple had. I had a successful business, a husband I adored and who adored me, and I wanted us to cement that even further by having a child.

At first, Graham wasn't against the idea, or at least he didn't seem to be. I didn't think anything of his requests to wait, to give it time. We were just married, we had just bought the house, my business needed me, and it wasn't the right time. All sensible reasons to put the plan for a baby on pause.

But as the years passed, our friends started to have families, and our relatives asked more and more if we were going to. I didn't like how he was pushing the idea back further and further. Stupidly, I let it pass, over and over until I didn't want to leave it anymore. There was no better time for it to happen. Life was good for us.

"Jesus, Andy. Why do you always do this?" He gestured angrily at me before turning his back on me and pulling the door of the wardrobe open harshly, ignoring me sitting on the bed.

"Do what?" I snapped.

"Things are going well for us, and here you are, ready to rock the fucking boat."

I felt the heat in my face building, along with my anger. "I want a family with you, Graham. Is that such a fucking hideous thing? Am I really the asshole in all this because I want what everyone else has and what everyone else does after being with someone and getting married?"

He glared at me, his look cutting me to ribbons. "Oh, right. So, we're meant to have a child to keep up with the Joneses, are we? 'Everyone else is doing it.' You sound like a fucking spoilt child."

"Fuck you, Graham," I spat. My heart was pounding, and I clenched my fists so hard my nails dug into my palms.

"Thanks for proving my point." His smugness cut into me from where he stood across the room from me. He may as well have been a million miles away. That was how it felt.

"I hate the way you do this. You always make it about you and what you want, and anything I want is something that needs to be compromised on. Not once in the eighteen years we've been together have you ever openly said you don't want children."

He sighed. He knew I was right. Sure, he had found

excuses for delaying it, but he hadn't said no, just 'not yet'. When we had first got together and talked about a future for us, he was the one who mentioned he would like to have a family.

"Well, I changed my mind." There was a harshness in his tone I had never heard before. A coldness that streaked across my heart.

"Would have been nice to fucking know that long ago."

"Well, I'm telling you now."

I really didn't understand how I could have had this all wrong. I thought we were on the same page about all this. I guess I couldn't have been more wrong. My heart sinks until it's practically in my feet. He might not have thought it, but this changed everything.

"Thanks, Graham. That's the first time in years you've been honest about it. I just wish you'd told me sooner."

He scoffed. "Does it really make that much of a difference? Can you honestly say what we have together isn't enough? That it isn't something we could continue regardless?" He tried to take my hand in his, and I pulled it back like his touch had scalded me.

Did he think so little of my feelings that he could try to sweet talk me into forgetting something so important to me? Something he knew was important from very early in our relationship. I had been honest, I had been accommodating, and I had let him push for his timetable in our lives. Was this how it would boil down in the end? I was the one who was meant to give up my wants and desires because they didn't match his?

The more I thought about it, the more I realised we might be at an impasse. Just as much as he couldn't expect me to put aside my wishes and goals, could I really expect him to do that? If I wasn't willing to do it, why should he?

"I can't be around you right now." I sighed.

I stood and moved to the wardrobe, took out the small suitcase that I used for business trips, and filled it with some clothes and some essentials.

"You're going to leave over this?" His resolve to make me come around to his thinking dissolved, and his eyes widened, taken aback that I felt so strongly about it.

I nodded. "I just need a day or two to think."

"Where are you going?"

"My sister's."

"Right."

Graham and my sister, Laura, had become more distant with each other lately. She would always have my back, and she had seen how happy being around my nieces and nephews made me. She knew how I felt about children of my own and had watched Graham push for that to be later and later, making me more miserable about it as time went on.

Sometimes, I thought he blamed her. She always encouraged me to be true to myself. She always had, but it only seemed to bother him when it came to this.

I walked out the front door, got into my car, and drove away. I made it as far as the end of the street and around the corner before needing to pull over. Tears streamed down my face. There was going to be no coming back from this one. My marriage was over.

Chapter Two
Andy

"ANDY, are you even listening to me?" Fiona says, poking me in the side as I stare at my phone.

"What?" I ask distractedly.

"I said, are you listening to me, but I think you just answered that one." I glance up at her. "What the hell is so interesting on Facebook?" She looks over the edge of my phone screen to see what's keeping my attention from the latest gossip on her love life.

I press the button on my phone to lock it before setting it back on the table in front of us. "Nothing. It's just a friend request from someone I've not heard from in years," I reply, trying to sound like it's the most natural thing in the world.

She gives me that look, and I know I'm already screwed. My mistake has been made and I've shared too much. She won't let this go now.

"Who?" She grins. "It's not an old flame, is it?"

"Oh, shut up, Fi!"

Don't get me wrong, I love Fiona. She's the best assistant a guy could have, but sometimes, as much as we're friends, she doesn't know when to stop.

"Ohh, it is an old flame!" She smirks, knowing full well I realise my mistake as much as she does. Yep, definitely not going to let this drop now. I'm fucked. I give a moment's thought to which is going to be the lesser of two evils; telling her now or letting her drag it out of me like it's some strange little game. Maybe the former is better.

Just tell her and get it over, Andy.

"Fine. Yes, it's an old flame. The oldest one there can be, as it happens." I sigh in defeat.

"Not the squaddie? The soul mate, love of your life, before he fucked off and you met Graham?"

Trust Fi to be as blunt as a brick to the side of the head. "Yes, that one. Only Chris wasn't a squaddie, he was in the Navy. Or at least he was the last time I saw him."

"How long has it been?" she asks a little too eagerly.

I think back on when I had last seen Chris Cooper. "I don't think I've seen him in about twenty years. And now he's sent me a friend request on Facebook."

"I see." She eyes me suspiciously. "Andy, if he's just an old flame, why are you so worked up about it already?"

I think about it, and I think about Chris. My mistake hasn't only been telling Fiona what I was so distracted over, it's the flurry of thoughts and feelings running around in my mind right now over the mere sight of his name and profile picture.

I haven't seen him or his sister in years. Zoe crosses my mind, and I wonder how things have turned out in life for the woman I always thought would end up being my sister-in-law. One day soon, I will have to look her up on Facebook and see if there's anything left of the embers of our friendship we can reignite.

Until then, I make a rash decision and delete Chris's friend request, trying to put the past out of my mind.

Chapter Three
Andy

THERE ARE times when I love my job. I love meeting new people, networking, the interactions... everything. But there are also times when I've been as busy as I have with this wedding expo when I can't wait to get back to the hotel, put on some jeans and a t-shirt, and go and enjoy the bar food and a quiet drink.

Fiona is down with the flu. She was meant to be with me. I've been training her to become a partner in the business to give me more time at home for when the plans I have come into fruition, but after she called me on Wednesday night, I told her to get her arse into bed and not move. The plan we had for the event was all but sorted, and it wouldn't be too much extra for me to do it solo. Tough, but not impossible. I had networked, chatted, sorted out some new contacts, generated fresh interest in the wedding planning business I run, and things were going well. I've earned the break tonight. Tomorrow, I'll head home, and while I can't wait to sleep in my own bed, part of me likes the company there is in strangers, especially at the minute. Nineteen years ago to the very day had been my wedding to Graham.

I'm not sure why, but this year, it's hitting me hard. I'm not dating, and I'm not any closer to starting the family I want. I'm trying not to be hard on myself, but at the moment, it's hard not to feel like a failure.

I think about it a little more as I check my work emails and distract myself from the reality of my surrogate recently going through what has cost me the last of my savings. Our third attempt at conception has just been done. I've been doing my best not to think about the fact that I might need to get a loan to try more. That I might have to look into adoption instead. It's all a mass of things running around in my head.

I need to put the turmoil of it all out of my head. I need to make the most of having one more night to avoid it. I grab my phone, my room key card, and my business credit card, and leave my room for the bar.

I settle into the little nook in the corner I found the first night and quietly enjoy a glass of red wine while I watch the latest match in the Rugby Union Six Nations. England is uncharacteristically kicking the ass of Wales, something I'll have great fun teasing Fiona about later when I phone her to tell her how it went today. I lose myself in the sights of big, strapping men running about a pitch, being rough as fuck with each other while attempting to score. It reminds me of Graham and all those cold Saturdays spent watching him play rugby for his university team, and the hot baths and sports massages that followed. Damn, I need to have a long wank later. I'm horny as hell and I need to take the edge off.

By the time the match is over, my glass is empty, and I head to the bar to order myself some food and another glass of wine. The bar is a little busier than usual, but I assume that's because it's a Friday night in a vibrant town. I wait to get the attention of the girl behind the bar.

I'm aware of a man standing beside me, and I'm about to order when the girl at the bar walks straight past me to the man, serving him first. I've never been one to shy away from telling someone they're wrong, and this certainly isn't the time for me to start. I'm hangry, and I turn to face the miserable, queue-jumping bastard.

"Uh, excuse me?" I start, but when the face who dared to take my place in the bar queue hierarchy turns to face me, I'm floored. A sentiment mirrored in the expression of said bastard. In an instant, my disgust at his behaviour melts, and it's replaced with an awareness of the tingling running through every inch of my body.

Of course, I'm face-to-face with none other than Chris fucking Cooper. All I can think about to distract me from the betrayal of my body's reaction to him is how Fiona is going to have a shit fit when she hears the latest feedback I have from the expo.

Chapter Four
Andy

19 years ago

THIS COULD NOT BE HAPPENING. *He'd better be dying to have stood me up like this.*

I stormed to Chris's house and banged repeatedly on his front door. When Mrs Cooper finally answered, I barrelled past her, racing upstairs to find him.

"Chris!" I called, lunging through his bedroom door.

"Andy! He's not here!" she told me as she entered his room, finally catching up with me.

"Where is he?"

His mum moved towards me and put her hand on my arm. "He's gone, love." The regretful tone of her voice was initially lost on me.

"Gone where? When will he be back?"

Mrs Cooper looked at me sadly; I could see the pity on her face. "He's gone away for a while, love. He won't be back for quite some time."

The room started to swim. "What do you mean he'll not be back for a while? Where... where is he?"

"He's not coming back, Andy, love."

No. This could not be happening. I loved him. He was my soulmate. He couldn't just leave me; he wouldn't. I pushed past his mum, ran down the stairs, and back out the front door.

Chris's sister—my best friend, Zoe—called out after me. "Andy, wait!"

I paused to wipe the tears from my eyes and the snot from under my nose before turning to look at her.

"He joined the Navy." Her voice was flat and detached. "I told that prick you deserved better. I told him he would get himself killed over his idiotic, pig-headed pride. But my brother is a twat, and he wouldn't listen." She put her hand on my arm, her eyes almost brimming over with tears. "I'm so sorry, sweetie. I tried to talk him out of it, but he thinks he has something to prove."

This had to be a nightmare. Any moment, I would wake up and things would be different.

I pulled my phone from my pocket and scrolled to Chris's number, hitting call. A tone sounded in my ear and a voice announced, 'The number you have dialled has not been recognised'. My eyes burned. I cancelled the call and typed out his number manually, just in case.

'The number you have dialled has not been recognised.'

Zoe stood in silence, looking at me as I crumbled. I felt her empathy, but I also felt her awkwardness. After all, what could be said to the friend whose heart her brother broke, leaving her and her and their family to explain it? I tried his number one last time.

"He changed it. He thought it was better that way."

"No!" I shouted and took off running.

"Andy, wait!" Zoe called after me.

But I couldn't stop. I didn't know where I was going.

Away from there; away from the truth, perhaps. I couldn't sit there and listen to my best friend try to comfort me when her brother was the one who had done it. I needed to escape from the overwhelming tidal wave of heartbreak threatening to swallow me whole. Chris was gone. I didn't know where, I didn't know how long he would be gone, and I had no way of contacting him anymore. It was over. Everything we had planned to do together now and in the future was apparently worth nothing to him. Just like I was. The thought made me stumble, and I crashed to the pavement on my knees. My embarrassment was only amplified by a guy I knew from school witnessing the whole horrific event. He rushed over to help me up.

"Jesus. Are you okay?" he asked as he put his arm around me and pulled me off the ground.

"I'm okay." My face burned. I accepted his help as he manoeuvred me to a bench.

"That knee looks bad." He pulled a tissue from his pocket. "It's clean," he added, dabbing the nasty graze on my leg. "Andy, right?"

I nodded, my eyes stinging from the myriad of emotions surging through me. Heartbreak. Embarrassment. The pain in my knee.

"I'm..." he started.

"Graham. I know."

A small smile graced his lips. "My mum is a nurse. She has a great first aid kit in the house. It's just over there. Can you make it that far?" He pointed to the house a few doors down, and I nodded.

"Maybe you'll tell me what happened over a cup of tea?" He smiled, putting his arm around me and helping me hobble over to his house for some tea and sympathy.

"*What the hell did you think would happen, Chris? It's been nine fucking years!*" *I growled.*

He sat on one of the seats in the ballroom that would be holding my wedding reception, his head in his hands, looking like his world had just fallen apart. Maybe it had, but I pushed that thought out of my head.

Nope. Not my problem. I wasn't the one to leave.

"*Fuck! I don't know, Andy. I guess part of me didn't think that far ahead. I guess I always had this mental image of a great reunion where I come back to find you still here, single, waiting...*" *His voice trailed off, and I stared at him.*

"*Are you for real? You thought you would leave me without a word or reason, and that I would somehow be sitting here pining away for you? Waiting for your glorious return with open arms?*"

He stood, ready to fight his side. "I know I didn't say anything. I know I just left. I didn't think I was fucking good enough, okay? I didn't think I was the man you needed, and I left to become something more. To make myself the kind of man you deserved."

"*What I deserved, Chris, was a boyfriend who didn't just up and leave and break my fucking heart. What I deserved was, at the very least, an explanation of where the hell you were going! Why the fuck are you even here?*"

"*Zoe called me and said...*"

I cut him off. "I should have known it wasn't a coincidence that you would come back to me now!" I would be having words with my best friend later. Telling her idiot brother about what I was doing was not what I needed right then.

He started to move towards me and took my hand. I

snatched it away. I didn't want him touching me. He left me, and I was supposed to be happy he was back? I couldn't believe how ridiculous he was being.

"Andy," he pleaded.

I can't do this; it's not fair. *I was getting married in three days. Graham had been my rock when I felt so lost. He looked after me when Chris left, and he grew into more. He deserved better than this. I couldn't drop him so close to the ceremony and go back to the idiot who left me. My heart ached because I would have been lying if I didn't admit that part of my heart would always belong to Chris Cooper. But I wasn't the kind of person to just walk away from someone I loved. I couldn't do that to Graham.*

"Chris, you tore my heart out. You were my whole world, and you disappeared without a trace. Graham was there for me. Graham put me back together. Graham would never leave me like you did."

"So, he's safe?" Chris bit.

I stormed towards him, my finger up in his face. I wanted to scream at him. I wanted to slap him. Instead, I shouted, "Don't you ever put him down. He might not be what you were to me, but he's still better than you. He would never treat me like you did." *My finger punctuated my words.*

Chris grabbed my wrist and pulled me against him.

This was emotional overload. I wanted to push him away, and before I got the chance to process it, his mouth was on mine. Instinctively, I responded, the last decade temporarily drifting away. My body moulded against him, tasted his tongue in my mouth, and all I could think of was Graham and the betrayal I was committing.

I pushed Chris off me with everything I had. My hand came across his face and straight to cover my own mouth in shock at my reaction to both him and what I just did. "Get the fuck out of here, Chris."

His lips parted. I knew that look. He thought about what to say, but then decided against it.

His hands were stuffed into the pockets of his jeans, his head hanging when he walked away. As he did, he bumped into Graham. "Sorry," he muttered.

"My bad," Graham replied.

Chris was gone. Again. Graham walked over, wrapped his arms around me, and kissed my forehead. Right then and there, I was split down the middle. Part of me belonged to Chris, and part of me belonged to Graham. I wasn't sure that would ever change.

Chapter Five
Andy

"Andy?" My name just rolls off his tongue, and the skin prickles at the back of my neck. His voice is older; a richer baritone than when I last saw him. He's taller than I remember. His eyes haven't lost a bit of that cheeky sparkle they had and are still a gorgeous chocolate brown you could easily lose yourself in by gazing into them for too long. I do, in fact, for a brief second, do exactly that, and I'm sure I must be blushing a little when I snap out of it and look at him.

"Fucking hell. Chris Cooper." I attempt to smile at him, but then overthink it. I'm sure I must look like a right twat. Before I have time to overthink that too and ask myself why I care if a man I haven't heard from in decades thinks I'm a twat, his arms are around me. He pulls me close against him.

"Christ, I haven't seen you in years," he murmurs against my neck.

Alarm bells are going off in my body and mind, already dragging me in two different directions. I feel it.

I melt into his hug, and his body gratefully accepts it.

Every inch of me is humming with energy, and so much of me wants to let whatever it is go wherever the fuck it's going. On the other side of that equation, my brain is screaming out to me and asking what the hell I think I'm doing. This is the man who broke my heart. This is the man who walked away from me, only to walk back in later and try to fuck with me all over again. I shouldn't be reacting to him like this.

That side wins this round. I pull back from Chris's hug, and for a split-second, I swear I see disappointment flash across his features. His eyes burn into me, and I feel them everywhere.

"So," I say, attempting to diffuse the situation. I need to encourage some kind of normal, friendly, innocent chitchat between us, instead of this sexually charged nuke threatening to implode and wipe out everyone in its wake.

"Can I get you a drink?"

"What have you been up to?"

We blurt the words in unison. The tension is broken, and we settle a little.

"Thanks. I'd love a glass of Rioja." I smile at him. He motions to the same bar wench who had ignored me in favour of him just minutes before and orders both of us a drink.

"Did you eat?" he asks. I tell him no and explain I was about to order when he so rudely interrupted. He smiles at me, and I feel the tension sneaking back in, only this time it's a little different. It's strangely exciting, a bare-naked thrill.

I tell Chris the food I want, and he puts in the order before paying and moving back to me.

"Where were you sitting?" he asks, and I motion for him to follow me back to my little isolated nook. The skin on my neck is prickling again, and I can sense his eyes on me. No one else is around where I've been sitting. I think about how I'm about to be tucked into a corner with a man who makes my body hum with just his presence.

I am so screwed.

Chapter Six
Chris

"So, how long have you been married to... Gavin, wasn't it?" I ask.

"Graham," he corrects. It's not a name I ever forgot, but I didn't want to give Andy the satisfaction of knowing that.

"Oh, yeah. Graham. Sorry."

He smirks, and I can tell he's feeling the victory in me seeming jealous. I'll let him have that one.

"Actually, we've been divorced for about two years now."

I know I shouldn't be happy about that, but something inside me just can't help it. I don't want Andy to be with anyone else. I never have.

"Sorry," I say.

He nods, and I can feel the something unsaid. There's something more he wants to add, but whatever it is, he stops himself.

"What about you?" he asks.

"Still single," I tell him, and I almost think I can see relief on his beautiful features.

"How come?"

"Honestly?" I shrug. "Because I once had the perfect man, and I lost him, and since then, no one else has ever measured up."

"Oh, right," he says, and I can tell he's trying to sound nonchalant.

I know he wants to ask who he was. By the look on his face, it appears as though he's about to query that, and then I see him realise.

Yes, Andy. You.

"Ohhh. Look, Chris, I–" he starts, and I take his hand.

"No, don't. I don't mean it like that. I knew you were married, believe me. It's why I stayed away the second time, after I saw you, I mean. Christ, I've never been able to hide anything from you, have I?" My thumb rubs over the back of his hand, and he looks at it, then at me. There's this loaded moment when that pull towards him starts in my chest. Without warning, he yanks his hand from mine like I've gone too far, and I regret it instantly.

Both of us sit in silence. He grabs his glass of wine and knocks it back in one long gulp. I take the glass from him and get up. "Let me get you another," I mumble almost bashfully and walk away to the bar.

When I get back from the bar, something has changed a little. Time passes, drinks flow, and we settle into a comfortable patter with each other. We talk about what we do and almost everything that has happened in the nineteen years that have passed since we saw each other.

Andy tells me about the divorce. I let him talk. I drink in the sound of his voice that I've missed all these years. I know I should probably tell him about the most recent developments in my life, but announcing that my sister died of cancer and I'm now the guardian of my seven-month-old niece feels like it would somehow mar the moment.

So instead, I keep the conversation about him, and I drink a little more. The more I drink, the flirtier I get. The occasional hand on his knee when I laugh at something he says. I can see it happening, and as much as I know I should pull it back, I'm not sure I want to.

He catches me in a look. "What?" he asks with a smirk.

"I've missed you, Andy." I can hear the regret in my voice. I hadn't intended for it to come out so obviously.

Andy stares at me. I want him to smile at my confession. I want him to admit he's missed me too, but I know he won't.

"Sorry. I didn't mean to make you uncomfortable again. I don't mean to spoil this," I say, gesturing between us.

He grabs my hand this time. "No! No... you haven't," he reassures me, and instead of letting go of him, I let our hands drop into the space between us, our fingers naturally entwining. He looks down at them and then back up at me. Absently, my thumb traces over the back of his hand. I squeeze his fingers and the pull starts. Suddenly, his face moves towards mine, and instead of moving away, I help close the gap between us. Seconds stretch out as my body tingles, waiting for that moment until his lips touch mine.

His phone rings. I look down at it and see his sister's name flashing on the screen.

Well, shit.

Chapter Seven
Andy

"Sorry about that," I say as I plonk my arse back down onto the seat beside him.

"No, it's fine," he says with a smile that doesn't quite reach his eyes.

"She was just checking on me, given that it would have been my wedding anniversary."

"Andy, she's your sister. Your family is allowed to call without you needing to explain to me."

There's an edge to his tone, and my heart sinks a little with regret. He had been about to kiss me, and what's more, I had been about to kiss him back. I'd wanted to. Hell, I still want to. But fate intervened again. If I were at all superstitious, I might take it personally.

"I know. But... I... I think I've had too much to drink after a long day. Maybe I should just go up to my room and head to bed." I sigh.

I watch him as he fights with himself over what to say next. "I'll walk up with you. To *my* room, I mean."

Another flood of disappointment washes over me. I shouldn't want him; I shouldn't be as turned on as I am. But there's something about Chris Cooper that does what it has always done. It speaks to my soul. It whispers to every last inch of me, particularly my cock.

"Okay," I murmur and stand up. The alcohol mixes with my neediness, and I stumble. Chris's hand is instantly at the small of my back to steady me against him.

"Uh, thanks," I say, pulling myself back from him, trying to take the hint that fate has given me and have some common sense, even if I no longer have decency. His hand slips from its hold of me, and he motions for me to lead the way. Slowly and carefully, I walk over to the elevators.

The last of the crowd from the elevator leaves, and there's just Chris and me getting in.

"What floor?" he asks me, his fingers hovering over the buttons.

"Six," I tell him.

He raises an eyebrow. "Me too. Funny coincidence."

I can't breathe anymore. I'm holding it because, if I let it out, I worry that he'll understand how nervous I am that he's got me wanting more, and I'll give myself away. So, I stand here, thinking about him being on the same floor as me. Thinking about the fact that he might be in the room next door, and I wait.

The lift arrives on the sixth floor, and I head out of it, letting out my breath as I do. Chris follows me. "Are you down here too?" I ask.

"Just a bit further."

I stop outside 606. "This is me," I say and fish the key card out of my back pocket. I put it into the little slot about twenty different ways, and it refuses to open the bloody door. Again, his hands are on mine.

"Give it here." He smirks.

I can't say anything. I'm too busy thinking about him

touching me again, and how there's a nice big bed on the other side of this door.

Chris puts the key card in the lock, pulls it out, and the green light flashes instantly. He pushes the door open, puts the card into the little slot on the wall, and flicks on the light. "You go and get some sleep," he tells me.

"Thank you." I smile at him. We pause, staring at each other, static swimming in the air around us.

"It really was lovely to see you again, Andy." He smiles at me. "Sweet dreams."

He pulls the door closed behind him, leaving me standing here. Hesitancy and yearning battle in my body. I want to go after him. I want to at least find out his room number, but I find myself rooted to the spot. Minutes pass, and I realise it's too late.

I flop on the bed, kick off my shoes, and grab the TV remote from the bedside table. At least I can view my blues away with some *Real Housewives of Orange County*. I sigh. The frustration won't do me any harm. My life is complicated enough with everything that's happened over the last few weeks.

I'm just about comfortable when there's a knock on my room door. I sigh, get up off the bed, and stomp over to it. I pull it open with a swift tug, and a split-second later, my body is engulfed by another's. Lips are on mine, and the second they touch me, that familiar feeling creeps all over me.

Chris. Chris's lips are on mine. Chris's hands have just cupped my arse. Chris's tongue is slipping between my lips and teasing my own.

Our kiss deepens as the intensity of the feelings I've been hiding from push to the surface after decades. I pull him hard against me and grab at the back of his t-shirt; I need to find his skin beneath it. When I do, I'm rewarded with a moan against my lips, his hips rocking against me, his hands sliding up my back and pulling me against him just as hard.

My head swims, and he pries his mouth from mine. "I'm sorry, Andy. I just... I had to fucking kiss you."

I can't fight it anymore. "Fuck, I've missed you," I tell him, and his lips collide with mine again.

Now, I don't care. Fuck the consequences. In this moment, I've never wanted anything more. In this moment, Chris Cooper has me utterly tempted. I might regret this in the morning. It might make the plan I made for my life a year or so ago more complicated, but this is *Chris*, and the same pull that has always been there draws me in still.

I just need to be with him.

Chapter Eight
Chris

My life is more complicated now than it has ever been, but the second I saw Andy, the years disappeared. Everything I felt for him all those years ago came flooding back. Fresh and in full, rich technicolour.

I make it as far as my room, but instantly regret not doing *something*. I think about it, and overthink it, and pace back and forth just inside the doorway until I decide I can't leave it like this. It's Andy Reece, the man who has been in my heart for my whole adult life, and complicated or not, I can't let this chance fly by.

I pocket my door key card, stomp straight back down the hallway to Andy's door, and give it a tentative knock.

Seconds later, it swings open with some force, and this time, I don't hesitate. I move into his space, my hands slide around his waist, I pull him to me, and my mouth engulfs his. There's a fraction of a moment where I feel him taking the time to process what's happening, but then he returns my kiss, fierce and with need. My hands slide over his arse, and I pull his hips against mine.

He returns my actions, pulling me hard against him. He

grabs at the back of my t-shirt, his fingers finding my skin beneath it. I moan against his mouth and can't help but rock my hips against his, my hands roaming over his back, holding him as tight against me as I can.

I've missed this man for two decades, and I need to pour out everything at once, just in case I never get the chance to do it again. He can never doubt that for those twenty-odd years, he was on my mind. I'm breathless when I pry my mouth from his to explain myself and draw breath. "I'm sorry, Andy. I just... I had to fucking kiss you."

"Fuck, I've missed you," he replies, and I take it as an invitation, colliding my mouth with his all over again.

He's hungrier for my attention now, and I need to lavish him with all the attention he's been missing out on. No matter what else happens between us, he's going to know I need him, and I've never stopped wanting him.

My t-shirt is the first thing to hit the floor. I'm amazed at the pure lust that crosses Andy's features when he looks at me. It's a way I've not been looked at in years. The desire, the attraction, the pure want; I've missed how he looks at me.

I hold my breath when his hands run over every inch of my chest and shoulders. I look down and watch the movement of his fingertips as they brush through my chest hair, just like he loved to do all those years ago. There's more of it now than when we were teenagers, and I'm more muscular too; one of the side effects of having been in the Navy. I've kept myself in shape ever since.

Every last part of me is crying out for all of him. It's like some strange floodgate has been opened after years of being pent-up and denied. I need Andy right now more than I need air.

Craving skin-on-skin contact with him, I grab the hem

of his t-shirt and pull it over his head, discarding it to the floor along with mine. I feast on the sight of him. Every bare inch of his torso is a delight to behold. He's carrying a little more weight than before, but it's damn near perfection on him. He's a little hairier himself. He's gone from nothing to a light dusting of hair across his body.

My hand runs over his chest, grabbing at his flesh, and my mouth descends to follow my hand, kissing the exposed skin. I'm starting to think I'm dreaming. I can't believe I'm back here, touching Andy, seeing him like this. Christ, if I am dreaming, I hope to fuck I never wake up. This is perfection.

My hands slide around his body to his back, and I pull him against my mouth as I encircle one of his nipples with my mouth.

He gasps at the contact, and his hand cups the back of my head. "Fuck, Chris."

In a rush of want at the sound of his exclamation, I need more of him. I move back upwards over his body, and my mouth skims his lips as my hands lazily trail down towards his backside. Goosebumps prickle over his skin as my mouth traces across his jaw to his neck. I feel like a man who has just won the lottery.

A long moan falls from his lips as I dip my head again and enclose his other nipple in my mouth. Again, his hands find the back of my head, holding me exactly where he wants me, nuzzling against him, and I pull him harder into my mouth. I break contact with him only briefly to swap to his other nipple.

"Oh, fuck, Chris!" he moans.

I look up at him, and when his eyes meet mine, I witness the pure, unadulterated lust reflected in them. In that instant, the entire world disappears. Nothing else exists but Andy and me.

"You are even better than I remember," I tell him, letting the words wash over him, hoping he knows how true they are. I stand and look at him, pulling him against me again. I've always wanted to see him again, and I never dreamed it would happen, or that it would end up like this. I lower my face to his, my lips brushing against his mouth lightly, making him need more.

Andy cups my face in his hands, and a day's worth of scruff prickles against his palms. "Nineteen years wear well on you," he tells me, and I'm overwhelmed by the need I have for him.

Instead of trying to say words that just won't form, I put my mouth on his and run my hands over his bare back.

As our kiss deepens, his hands roam down to my ass, where he grabs a handful. My hips gain a mind of their own and roll against his grasp. Andy responds by pulling me harder against him. I know he can feel how hard I am through our jeans. Hell, I can feel how hard he is for me too, and I'm also aware we're both wearing far too many clothes.

He wraps a leg around my hip. I know he needs more contact with me against all the right places, and instinctively, I reassign a hand from his ass to hold his leg. I trace my fingers firmly along his thigh, and the need for more and the heady passion of our kissing make my head spin. I'm overwhelmed. I'm out of control. I am so turned on right now that I could spontaneously combust.

Suddenly, Andy pushes me back. I let his leg drop so he can get his foot on the floor.

"What's wrong?" I ask, trying to sound casual, while inside I'm praying he isn't about to change his mind. Maybe he can't forgive me for what I did all those years ago. God knows it took a long time for me to make my peace with it, even if I didn't actually forgive myself.

He holds up a hand and stops me from saying more. "Give me a second. It's all good. I'm just a little too..." His voice trails off, unable to explain what he means.

I steel myself for what's coming. "It's okay, Andy. You don't have to do this. I wouldn't want you to do anything you would regret."

I wouldn't regret this for a second, but if he needs to stop, then God help me, I'll collect my t-shirt from the floor and leave if he wants me to.

I pray that's not about to happen, but whatever he wants, that's the least I owe him after everything that's happened between us over the years.

Chapter Nine
Andy

I ᴋɴᴏᴡ he really means it. God bless Chris Cooper because I know if I tell him I can't do it, he'll leave. But I can't let that happen. It's not at all what I want. I look at him and shake my head. I know if I don't do what I'm about to do, that will be my regret. Walking away from this beautiful man is positively impossible. I just need a few seconds to take stock. To collect my thoughts and calm my nerves.

My nerves are still shot, but I can't *not* do this. I need to. I need to feel this. To feel him. Even if it's only for tonight.

Chris looks at me, and I can see a moment of disappointment flicker across his features. He thinks I've changed my mind.

I move towards him and grab his hands, then push him back towards the bed and make him sit. "Stop that thought," I tell him, then kiss his forehead. "This is happening, Chris. I want you more than I can tell you."

Backing away from him, I put my hands on the waistband of my jeans. Undoing the zipper, I let my gaze catch his as I slip out of the denim. He watches as more and more of my legs are exposed until I'm standing in front of him in just my briefs with the effect he's been having on me very apparent. Creeping back over to him, I pull him to his feet. I trace my hands over the front of his torso as he stands there, staring at me, watching my every move intently, letting me do whatever I want to.

My hands skim over the waistband of his jeans. I undo his fly and sink to my knees in front of him as I slide them down his thighs.

"Fuck, Andy. You have no idea what a sight you are down on your knees," he breathes, as I run my hands down his outer thighs, slowly undressing him.

I look up at him, lick my lips, and say, "Oh, I think I might," before placing a kiss on his hard cock through his boxers.

"Fuck!" His cock bobs in shock at the contact. I stare at the sight of him tenting his underwear, craving a taste of him. I help him out of his jeans and boots and look up at him. His breathing has quickened, and he stares at me with an intensity I feel straight through to my cock.

I run my hand up his inner thigh. While returning the intensity of his look, my finger skims over the bottom of his balls, and I slip it between his legs to rub along the crack of his firm arse.

"Get in the middle of the bed," I command, letting my hand fall from between his legs so he can move.

Chris walks to the side of the bed and looks at me. I know what he's doing as he holds my gaze. He waits for my reaction and slides his boxers down his legs, gets onto the bed, and grins at me. I know my mouth has fallen open to an 'o', but it's difficult not to with the sight of such flagrant masculinity standing to attention directly in front of me.

I repeat his exclamation from earlier. "Fuck!" I stare at his cock; it's bigger than I remember. For a split-second, I wonder if it's that my memory of it has lessened, or if it actually has grown over the years.

I snap myself out of my pondering and gaze over him lying on the bed, ready for the taking. I know exactly what I want to do with him.

"Spread your legs, Chris," I tell him, surprised at the heat in my voice. The confidence I had long forgotten pours forth as I put my knee on the foot of the bed and move towards him.

His legs part and allow me the space to get in between them. Like a hunter stalking his prey, I keep what I want firmly in my sights as I creep slowly towards him.

I place my lips on the side of his right calf, and he moves a little, putting his hands behind his head like he's about to relax and enjoy the show I'm putting on for him. I give a little smile as I kiss up towards his knee and wonder how long his hands will stay where they are once I start doing what I plan to.

Once I reach his right knee, I kiss from his left calf up to his knee, and then softly kiss over his inner thigh until I hit just below his balls. Swapping back to the right leg, I climb higher in a trail of kisses until I'm, again, just under his balls.

I stare directly at him, my tongue caressing the underside of his scrotum. He gasps, his cock jumping against his stomach, begging me for attention. I run my hands firmly over his thighs as I take one of his balls into my mouth and suck gently.

Chris groans, but his eyes never leave mine. I know he's drinking in the sight of me kneeling, sprawled out between his legs, my hands on his skin and my tongue almost on the prize.

I can't resist anymore. I reach forward and lick the

length of his cock, from his balls, to the tip of his thick head. His breath stutters out of his body on a staccato exhalation. I'm flooded with memories of how good it sounds to hear this man moaning because of my mouth on his dick and some of the other tricks I had up my naïve little sleeves way back when.

I repeat the action, and he hisses. "Fuck, Andy. Stop teasing me and do it right," he begs.

I look at him with a grin and sink my lips over the head of his cock, lifting it with my hand to get a better angle to take him all in my mouth. I stare at him intently and slowly descend my mouth over his rock-hard length. A long moan erupts from Chris as I do.

"Fuck. Your mouth is more perfect than I recall," he groans, his hand touching my face and then running through my hair. When he hits the back of my throat for the first time, his hand knots in my hair, and he uses it to encourage my pace. I pull away from him and let him almost fall from my mouth before sinking over him once again. This time, his hips shift, and he pushes deeper, the head of his cock pushing against my gag reflex. He stares at me intently.

"Christ, you look good with my dick in your mouth!" Chris groans.

I run my hand over his balls, and his eyes roll and close as he sucks in a breath. I bob my head up and down, sliding him in and out of my mouth, caressing him as I do.

I can't help but delight in the sweet sounds Chris is making under my influence. I gather some saliva in my mouth and soak my index finger before I run my tongue over the head of his cock. At the same time, I slip my slippery index finger between his ass cheeks, hovering over his arsehole.

The next time the tip of his length hits the back of my throat, I push my digit against that ring of muscle, feeling it give way. As I rise and sink again on his dick, I start thrusting into him, matching the movements of my mouth, pushing him more and more, closer and closer with every move I make.

I look up at him and, again, his eyes lock on mine. The dampness on the front of my briefs rubs against my hard cock from where my pre-cum has leaked out of me, making me feel like a teenager again. Still, I'm spurred on by the intensity of his gaze.

Chris watches me working him over. His breathing grows shallow, and his fist tightens harder in my hair. He pulls slightly, not letting me take his full length to the back of my throat.

"You need to stop," he warns. The thought of him close to climax thrills me and makes me want to taste him all the more. "Andy, I need to be inside you. God, after twenty years, I need to come inside you."

His stare pierces through me and I lick his dick before letting it slip from between my lips and slap back down on his taut stomach.

I remove my finger from his ass, and Chris grabs my hand and slips my index finger between his lips, sucking himself from my digits.

"Nice little trick." He smirks when he's done.

I grin. "I may have learned a few things over the years."

He tucks his hands under my arms and pulls me up over his body, so our faces are just inches apart.

"Oh, yeah?" he whispers against my lips as his mouth hovers over mine, threatening to claim it.

"Yeah." I grin again, and Chris's lips crush against mine,

his arms pulling me tight against him. Every inch of him is pressed hard against every inch of me.

Without me realising what he's up to, Chris flips us so I'm beneath him. "My turn," he tells me, and sinks down over my torso, placing his knee between my legs and pushing them apart.

When he finally gets to where he wants to be, Chris is resting with a shoulder against each of my inner thighs. I gaze down and see his intense stare looking up at me. Without allowing me the chance to process what's about to happen, he slides my briefs down my legs, casts them aside, and pushes my knees up. His tongue finds its way between my buttocks and licks over my arsehole.

"I've fucking dreamt about tasting you again," he murmurs against my taint before sinking his long, firm tongue inside me.

Holy fucking shit. Chris Cooper's tongue is fucking my arse.

Uhhh, is the only 'word' I have for him in that moment. Apparently, I'm not the only one who has learned some skills in the last almost twenty years.

Fucking Chris Cooper. Damn.

Chapter Ten
Andy

I'VE BEEN hard and turned on since he jumped the queue in front of me at the bar. Kissing him and tasting him has only made the situation worse, and within what must be only thirty seconds of Chris's tongue sliding into my arse, I need more. He needs to be inside me properly. His mouth is amazing, but I'm so fucking needy for more, and as I'm about to beg, he slides a finger inside me to finger fuck me, his hand angled at just the right position to rub against my P-spot with every thrust.

I watch as he smirks up at me. He clearly hasn't forgotten how my body reacts any more than I've forgotten how his does. The sensations rush me all at once, and I close my eyes with a gasp. Colours dance across my eyelids, and a small amount of cum pools on my stomach.

"Oh, fuck, Chris," I breathe as I start to come down from my climax. He grins at me, clearly pleased with himself, and I swear it's the sexiest sight I've seen. A shiver goes through me, thinking of what he just did to me.

Chris flexes his finger against my P-spot once more, and again, I shiver, a soft moan escaping my lips.

"Fuck, I love that sound. I've missed hearing it," he says fondly.

"I've missed you making me do it."

At my admission, Chris once again sinks his mouth down over my sensitive cock, licking and sucking me. He adds a second finger to the thrusting he's begun with the first and alternates between stroking that little bunch of nerves inside me and sucking my cock.

A second orgasm builds quickly, and Chris stops sucking so as not to take me too far. I haven't felt so desired in a fucking long time.

Chris takes me through my second climax, prolonging the feeling with skilled licks of his tongue over my balls and flicks of his fingers. When he's sure I've come down again, he removes his fingers from inside me. I hiss at their loss, and Chris puts his fingers in his mouth, savouring my flavour.

"Fuck, I've missed your taste, Andy. You're fucking delicious," he says before sliding his index finger into his mouth and sucking on it.

The man is pure sex, and I need more.

Chris moves back over my stomach, kissing my skin. He stops at my nipples to give them extra attention, and I know it won't be long before he'll have me coming again, hopefully this time with him buried inside me.

By the time Chris makes it back to my mouth, I can feel his length between my thighs. The tip of his shaft slides between my buttocks, and we both hiss at the urgent need it starts within us.

"I need to be inside you, Andy," he breathes across my neck as he nibbles on the skin below my earlobe.

I'm overwhelmed with lust for this man. "I need you there," I admit and feel his cock bob against me.

"I don't have anything lube with me," he tells me in hushed confession.

"Shit," I say, then I remember I have a small jar of Vaseline on the bedside table. I don't think I've ever been happier to have had dry lips than I am at this moment.

He pops it open and spreads it over my arsehole, pushing a little inside with his finger before rubbing it all over his cock. I wrap my arms around his neck and hook my legs around his. The latter move pulls him against me, the head of his cock ready to sink into my willing arsehole if he were to flex his hips.

"Are you sure about this, Andy? Once I start, I won't be able to stop," he warns me.

"I know." I hold his gaze, making sure he knows exactly what I mean. "Please," I almost beg.

"Jesus, Andy." He sighs, his lips crushing against mine. His hips roll upwards, his cock sheathing itself within me in one steady move. We both moan at the feeling of his thick cock forcing me to stretch out and accommodate him.

"Oh, Chris!" I breathe against his lips when he rolls his hips, withdrawing a little from me before sinking back in even deeper.

"I've been waiting for this," Chris says, and I'm not sure if he means tonight or the past two decades. One thing is for sure.

Nothing has ever felt so right.

"I've needed it longer," I tell him.

"Not even possible," he argues, pulling back and thrusting in hard, his mouth finding my nipple.

I can't take it. It's like my nipple is directly wired to my cock, and the second Chris's mouth connects with it, I cry out his name.

"Fuck, Andy. I've missed being inside you."

His pace is slow and luxuriously teasing. Every nerve in my body is slowly engulfed by the sparks of passion he's igniting within me. His mouth leisurely surrounds first one nipple and then the next, his tongue flicking over them, driving me insane. I run my hands over his back.

Some things have very much changed over the last twenty years. Some things feel just as they always have. This moment is an amazing mix of the two. I feel like I've come home. That single thought is all it takes to make it all seem too much and puts me into overload.

Chris's mouth is on mine, his hips moving faster now, his hands reaching between us and stroking my cock. I close my eyes and let the feelings wash over me. My moans and Chris's rising together let the neighbours know what's happening in my room. And damn if that thought doesn't tip me over.

"Oh, fuck! Yes, Andy. Come hard for me!" he encourages before kissing me fiercely. I know his climax is hitting right along with mine. He parts his lips from mine and the most incredible moan bursts forth as he comes hard inside me. More shivers vibrate through me in response, and I'm suddenly overcome with emotion. Years of anger, frustration, and longing melt away with the fading of my orgasm, and tears well up in the corners of my eyes.

He looks at me intently with an expression I know deep down inside is of pure love. I open my mouth to explain to Chris, but he captures my mouth with his. His thumb finds my tears to sweep them away as he balances himself against me.

He rolls his hips and pierces me with an earnest gaze, his mouth no longer on mine.

"I know," he says, cradling my face. "I feel it too."

More tears flood my eyes, and I feel like I'm going to be

utterly screwed in more ways than one by the time this night is over. Every emotion I've ever felt for Chris is circling my mind. I'm painfully aware that I never actually got over this man, and that feels like a vice around my chest. I love him still after all these years. I still hate him for all he did, leaving me to pick myself up, and I hate that it's all burst open and is raw all over again.

"Don't you dare drift away on me. I can see that mind of yours working overtime," Chris whispers and seizes my mouth with his, kissing me almost reverently as the bliss continues to roll over us. He gradually gets heavier against me, his arms no longer willing to support him. "I'll get off you." He sighs, exhausted, and I clutch him tight against me.

"Don't you dare move!" I growl. "Not yet. Lean on me. I don't care." Tentatively, he leans more of his weight on me.

Time slows, and I stroke his back, running my hand over his super short hair, our bodies still joined together in the most obvious place.

This is what home feels like, and I never want to lose it again.

I don't know how I will work this out. I don't know how to make sure that happens. I lie here, intertwined with Chris Cooper at an age when I can genuinely appreciate it, and it's divine.

Chapter Eleven
Chris

When I finally tuck myself in beside Andy, a few hours have passed. We must have dozed off in our sated state. I'm lying here, blissfully comfortable with my arm draped over his body, and I can hear his even breath as he sleeps beside me.

I glance over at him and can't help but smile.

"What?" he asks sleepily.

I bite back a little chuckle. "Nothing."

"Then why are you staring at me with a smirk on your face?"

I shake my head. "How do you even know that? Your eyes are still closed."

"I know you, Chris Cooper."

"Oh, is that so?"

He opens his eyes and looks at me. "Oh, I'm pretty sure I can still read you well enough." He smiles over his shoulder at me.

"Stubbornly determined still, huh?" I tease, smirking at him.

"Oi!" He laughs and elbows me in the ribs.

An '*uumph*' escapes from my lips. "And violent. Did I mention violent?" I can't help but keep being playful with him. I rub my hand over my ribs where his elbow made contact.

"Asshole."

"Oh, yeah, and rude!" I laugh, preparing myself for more banter. "I've missed you giving me shit, Andy."

He half fakes a sulk, and with a pout on his sexy mouth, he starts to get out of the bed when I grab him and pull him tight against me, manoeuvring myself to be slightly above him. I press my lips against his before he can get any more complaining out, my tongue snaking over his lips, begging entry to his mouth. He smiles against me and licks me back in reply, penetrating my mouth with his tongue.

"Did I also forget to mention how fucking sexy you look when you're pissed at me?" I tell him as I hold his face in my hands, scanning over all of his features, memorising them in case this is all I'm going to get with him. I'm determined it won't be, but just in case.

He glares at me, and I can tell he's fighting a hint of a smile. "Yes, you might have missed that one too."

I nod. "Shame, because you really are so fucking hot when you're pretending to be mad at me."

He glares at me some more, and I tilt my hips against him, my hardness pressed against him in the hope that he realises how much I'm not kidding. He *is* sexy as hell when he's pissed at me.

"Well, if I had known that, I would have shown you how annoyed I was at you when you fucked off to the Navy," he chides.

That little outburst takes me by surprise; while I was expecting it to come up, but not right at this moment. "I was wondering when you would bring that up." Swallowing down a sigh and I move back to let him roll away from me if he wants to.

"This isn't me going over it. This is just me wanting the chance to say how much it hurt me. I thought you were the one, Chris, and you left me."

Flopping down on the bed beside him. Defeated, my heart sinks, and the guilt of two decades washes over me. I run my hands over my face. "I know I did, Andy." Glancing regretfully in his direction, I add, "And when I found out you were getting married, it shredded my heart. I knew I would regret my choice forever."

His next words take my breath away. "I would have left him if you had asked me to."

"Shit, Andy. I'm so sorry." The words aren't enough. I should have asked him. I should have fought harder for him. I should have never fucking left him in the first place. But my stupid ego had me thinking I wasn't enough and that I needed to be something more than I was.

"You're an idiot. You always have been."

"Andy," I growl, his words cutting me.

He puts his hand on my mouth. "No. You're going to hear me out on this one, Mister. I don't know if you asking me to leave him would have been a smart move. I wanted you to, and I probably would have because you asked me. As angry as I was with you then, I could never deny the feelings I've always had for you. But I believe life happens how it's meant to. Graham wasn't a bad man. We had, for the most part, a good marriage. We just wanted to go in different directions in the end. But I'm older now, and things have changed in what I want and how I think."

"I'm not asking you to want me," I admit softly, hearing the vulnerable edge in my voice.

Andy rolls towards me. He looks at me with sadness and strokes my cheek. "It's been twenty years."

I swallow hard, thinking about my next comment carefully. "Then why are you here?" I brace myself for the answer, not entirely sure what he's going to say or what I want him to say.

"Because it's you, and you're... you're you," he replies.

A small grin pulls on the edges of my mouth. I used to say those words to him when he asked me exactly what I saw in him. Why I loved him. The significance of his repetition of the line isn't lost on me. "Are you saying I'm irresistible?" I joke, lightening the mood a little.

He shakes his head and sighs, laughing. "You are incorrigible!"

"I am, but that's why you love me!" I grin.

Andy smiles back, but he doesn't answer, and I know that's because he knows I'm right. He does love me, and the truth is, I still love him. I always have, and we're idiots for wasting so much time we could have had together instead.

This time, it's Andy who changes the mood. He leans over me and finds my lips with his. I give in to the moment and pull him against me. I know he can feel me getting hard again—he is too—and I can't wait to be where I was always meant to be. Deep inside him.

Chapter Twelve
Andy

A FEW HOURS' sleep and a few orgasms later, it's morning. I wake again with Chris's arm draped over my body, and the rest of him is pressed against my back. I run my hand over his and press my ass back against him, loving how well we fit together.

His hand moves over my stomach, running up my torso until it lazily fiddles with what little chest hair I have. He nuzzles against my shoulder, nipping at my bare skin, his hard cock pressing against the crack of my arse. His fingers find my nipple, and I push my ass against him with a sigh. Chris nibbles harder on my shoulder, enticing a moan from me. His hand drops from my chest to my groin, and he runs his palm between my legs, over my cock. I grind back against him, and he sighs against my neck, sending a shiver of desire through me.

I slip my hand behind him and grab his buttocks as he grinds his cock along the length of my arse. He breaks contact with me, and I hear the tub of Vaseline open again. Moments later, he's reaching between us to position his cock against my asshole. He pushes himself against me, and his hand goes back to teasing pressure on my dick.

Chris rubs himself against my bum, pushing against it with his cock and the circling of his fingers. He gets me so hot for him that I push back against him. I want him. I want him in me... *again.* I'm engulfed by a primal need to have him own every inch of me before I must leave and go back to reality.

My eyes roll back in my head in response to the delicious burn that's going on with Chris's hands on me.

"Oh, God, Chris," I moan as I feel my muscles want to give in to his cock. He pulls back a fraction, just enough to have more pressure to push against me and for the tip of his cock to push inside me.

The overwhelming sensations slam into me as Chris fills me. There's a slight discomfort as he stretches me out to accommodate him, and fuck, it feels so good. I clench around him. I'm so incredibly turned on, and all I want him to do is take me harder.

Chris starts a rhythm that has him thrusting hard and deep with short strokes, pulling out almost too far before crashing back into me. He pushes against my p-spot with each thrust and, God, I want more and more of him.

Chris takes me to the edge of pleasure and over it again and again. The notion that I never came this often or as easily with Graham flickers guiltily through my mind for a moment, only to fade again as another thrust pulls me back into the moment.

This time, I cry out his name when my climax strikes. I whisper it over and over like it's a fucking prayer. I want Chris; want him deep inside me. I want to feel him flooding me, and I realise I'm going to have to ask him.

"Chris!" I breathlessly exclaim.

He plunges hard against my p-spot again and raises a long moan from me. "Fuck, Andy!"

"Oh, God. Fill me."

"Don't you feel filled?" he asks, pushing hard against me.

I do, but that's not the filled I mean, and I need to get enough clarity through the well-fucked fog that has captured my brain to get the words out.

"Fuck, Chris... I need your cum," I blurt.

A low, guttural moan is the only reply I get. Chris's hand grabs my hip, and he slams hard into me. I feel that first spurt of his cum as he unloads deep in my arse, and I can't help the smile that comes across my face.

We both come hard and lie on our sides, panting, as the ability to think rational thoughts, speak, or even move slowly returns to us.

Not for the first time, Chris's cock remains buried inside me afterwards, and I relish that feeling. There's no haste. It's not a job to walk away from once complete. He needs the connection with me as much as I need it from him.

I wriggle slightly, realising that, at some point, I will have to leave this bed. Chris's hand again pulls me tight against him. "Not yet."

I melt against him at his tone, which is sated yet possessive. He puts me at ease, and I want to prolong the bubble we exist in for as long as possible.

"I have to move," he murmurs against my back after a while. "I don't want to, but it'll be time to check out soon, and I need to have a shower and grab my stuff."

Reality washes over me, and when Chris pulls out of me, I mourn the loss even more. A shiver runs through me, and I suddenly feel the cool air of the room more harshly. I make a move to collect the covers and wrap them around myself when Chris takes my hand. "Come shower with me," he says and pulls me up, waiting for me to come with him.

I willingly leave the bed and accompany him to the bathroom. He kisses me softly and holds me tenderly against him. "This is the best way to start any day," he remarks as he adjusts the temperature of the water from the shower. "Get in." He holds the shower door open for me. I step in, and Chris gets into the shower behind me and closes the door.

I stand under the water, letting it wash over me, trying not to think about how this time with him is coming to an end. Chris moves behind me, pressing himself against me as he grabs a handful of body wash from the bottle in front of me.

"Put your hands up on the wall," he instructs me, and when I do, I'm blessed with the feeling of his soapy hands rubbing all over my form. Again, my emotions overwhelm me. I feel cared for in a way I didn't know I was missing. Lifting my head to the water flowing down over me, I put my face in it as the tears start to fall, ensuring they're unseen.

Chris carefully and lovingly washes over every inch of me, cupping my arse and my cock tenderly as he does. When he's finished paying me attention, I rub my hands over my face and grab the bottle of body wash to repeat the intimate act on him.

Once bathed, we move in silence. We dry ourselves, stealing glances at one another. We dress, and I feel the end coming closer and closer. I step into the bathroom to clean my teeth and steel myself for what's about to happen.

When I leave the bathroom again, Chris is dressed and standing, ready to go.

He moves towards me, his arms surround me, and he holds me tight against him. Again, for one last time, the world around us fades away, and all that exists is us in this embrace.

Chapter Thirteen
Andy

CHRIS LEFT AFTER THAT. He said he would come back and we could share a taxi to the train station together, but I just couldn't do it. Prolonging the agony of having to part company with him again, my already raw emotions would be shredded further, and not knowing where all this was going... it was a vulnerability I wasn't yet ready to reveal to him. Instead, I left before he got back.

I get on the train, put my case in the overhead storage, park my ass on my seat, and stare blankly out the window. Now more than ever, I wish I had his number. I already regret leaving. I already know I want more.

My phone vibrates and I glance down at it.

Chris Cooper
If you thought you could just walk away, you forget that I know you, Andy Reece. I put my number in your phone when you were in the bathroom and sent myself a message to get your number, just in case.

Relief washes over me. I haven't lost him yet. Truthfully, I have no fucking clue what is going to happen next. I have plans, and I don't know if I want to bring Chris into them. Do I pause those plans if the IVF hasn't worked yet and wait to see what happens between Chris and me? I'm not sure I can think about that right now. What I do know is that I'm feeling alive in a way that I haven't felt in a very long time, simply because I've seen him, and I'm filled with nervous excitement over the possibilities because I have a way to be in contact with him again. Everything else will have to be left to fate.

I hit reply to the waiting message.

Thank you xx

I hit send, returning my phone to my bag. I rethink my need to confess to him, pull my phone back out of my bag, and tap out another message.

My life is a little complicated at the minute, but no matter what, I'm glad I bumped into you. I'm glad I get to see you again, and I'm very glad you know me well enough to sneak your number into my phone xx

Just as the train starts to leave the station, I catch a glimpse of Chris standing on a different platform. He takes his phone from his pocket, looks at the screen, and grins. He taps out a reply before putting it back. My phone pings, and I glance down.

I'm not going anywhere this time. I'll see you again soon, Andy x

I smile when I read his words. I would love to believe them, but there's a fear deep inside me that if I blink, he'll be gone again. I might have just survived the last time, but I'm not sure if it's something I would be able to endure again. Whatever happens next, I know I have to be careful. I need to know I can trust him before I take it any further.

Chapter Fourteen
Chris

"Hello, son. Nice trip?" Mum asks as I walk into my kitchen and kiss her on the cheek.

"Not too bad, yeah." I smirk, thinking of what happened over the last few days. "Has she been a good girl for her nanna?" I smile at my seven-month-old niece as she plays happily on the floor.

She eyes me suspiciously. "You're looking chuffed with yourself."

I attempt to avoid her comment by walking around the breakfast bar to Hannah and scooping her up into my arms. She gives me a drooly grin. "Hello, my gorgeous girl. Did you miss Uncle Chris?"

I can feel Mum's gaze on the back of my neck. I know she knows something happened, and I'm very aware of the fact that she's not going to let it go until she knows what happened.

"What?" I smile, feigning innocence.

"Don't you 'what' me, Chris Cooper."

Morag Cooper has always been a stubborn woman with an uncanny ability to read her children. I could never get anything past her when I was a teenager, and even now, in my forties, the same thing still stands.

I give Hannah a kiss and pop her back down on her mat. I look at Mum and roll my eyes. "Fine. I had a bit of a blast from the past while I was in Birmingham."

Mum's brow creases, and she looks at me, waiting for me to put her out of her misery.

"It was Andy."

Mum's eyebrow goes up. "Andy Reece?"

I nod.

"Isn't he married now?"

I close my eyes and sigh. Is there nothing my mother doesn't know about?

"Divorced, actually. For about two years now."

"Did you tell him about Hannah and your sister?"

I shake my head.

Mum gives me *the* look. "No time for talking, huh?"

I shake my head in disgust. "Mother, I am not discussing *that* with you."

She laughs at me. "I'll take that as a yes, then. Are you going to see him again? You still have Zoe's letter for him, don't you?"

I nod. I haven't thought about anything else since I last saw him. "I really would like to. But we'll have to see how it goes. I'm in Portsmouth, he's in Basingstoke. It's not far, but with Hannah, it's much more complicated."

Mum nods in agreement. "You need to tell him, and soon. Don't go dicking the poor fella around like you did the last time, son. That wouldn't be fair."

I wince because she's right. I caused him hurt, and my mum got to see it first-hand.

"I know," I admit, defeated. I don't want to be the reason for Andy's hurt ever again.

I kiss Hannah's cheek and think about how my life looks nothing like I expected it to. But hopefully, I can now have it look a little more like I wanted it to all those years ago. For the first time in a while, I at least feel like I have a chance of having a little happiness after all.

Chapter Fifteen
Andy

I sɪᴛ at my desk and sigh. I feel like I've come back down to earth with a bump. I have a million and one new ideas to discuss with Fiona. Some interesting new trends came out of the expo, and I can't wait to implement them in some of the weddings we have coming up if the brides like them.

She catches me distracted and staring at my phone. "You're lost in that bloody phone again. Should I be asking why?"

Guiltily, I turn it face down and sigh. "No. Nothing going on."

She smirks at me. "You know I know when you're lying, right?"

I frown at her. "I met someone."

Fiona's face lights up. She's been on at me to see someone for a while now. She's right, of course, but I'm not about to tell her that. I do need to finally get off my arse and get on with my life. That was the whole point of the divorce, after all. Freedom to move on and get on with what I'm meant to be doing in life. And two years on, here I am. No man, no baby, and until the last few days, no prospects of either.

I hold my hand up to pause her thoughts. "It's not what you think, and I don't know what, if anything, will come of it."

Fiona opens her mouth in shock. "*You* had a one-night stand?" She puts her hand on her chest and mocks me with her exasperation. I swear, if she was wearing pearls, she would be clutching them.

"It wasn't like that. I know him. I've known him for years."

I can see the cogs in Fi's brain working overtime. "Not Graham!"

I shake my head. "Christ, no! This is someone I've known even longer than that."

She stares at me blankly.

I sigh. "Chris."

Fiona breaks out into a flurry of goldfish mouth movements and flapping hands. "You had a one-night stand with Chris Cooper, the man who left you as a teenager?"

Yeah, thanks, Fiona. Like I needed a reminder of that last part.

"Yes, that Chris. It was really nice, actually. We exchanged numbers, and we've sent a message or two since I got back."

We had sent more than one or two messages. Last night, there had been a lot of very raunchy text messages exchanged. It's a wonder my phone hadn't melted with the heat of the conversation. But there hadn't been much in the way of being able to see each other again.

"Nice?" Fi scoffs, breaking me from my thoughts. "Nice is not a word I have ever used for a man I've lusted after for years and finally got him in the sack."

I grimace. "Jesus, Fiona. You have such a crass way of putting things. It wasn't like that. And you're right, it wasn't nice. It was amazing. The best experience I've had in years."

Fiona grins at me. "So, when are you seeing him again?"

I shake my head. "Honestly, I don't know. He's not local anymore, so I'm not sure how it would work."

"You want it to, though, right?"

I can't help but nod. I really do want to see Chris again, and I would love to have something work out between us.

"He and I have history, Fi. And not all of it is good. I need to be sure he wouldn't do anything like that again."

"You're both a lot older now, though. Surely that was just a teenage bout of stupidity?"

I hope it was, but the truth is, I don't know how it will go this time around. It's definitely something for me to think about.

Chapter Sixteen
Chris

"CAN you keep Hannah for me again this weekend, Mum?" I ask once we get through the pleasantries of our phone call.

"Anytime, love. You know that. Where are you off to?"

I know what's coming after I admit where I'm going. "I'm going to Basingstoke."

There's a silence on the line, and I don't need to see my mum to know the look she has on her face.

"Don't say it, Mum," I say before she has a chance to get started. "I'm going to tell him. I promise. I have the letter here too."

"You'd better," she answered curtly.

I sigh. "I will."

We discuss the final logistics of when I will be dropping Hannah off and collecting her again. Mum finishes the call by reminding me that I really do need to tell Andy everything that's happened in my life in the two decades we were apart.

I set my phone on the coffee table and flop back on the sofa, thinking about everything that's happened that Andy needs to know. The small stuff. The big stuff. Zoe's death is definitely a big one, and it's sure to hit him hard because Zoe was his bridesmaid, along with his sister, Laura. Life had let them drift apart, especially as there was always a little resentment about the fact that she had been the one to tell me he was getting married. It all boiled down to trust I guess, and that is something which seemed to be in short supply between me and Andy.

Having a kid is another pretty big one, especially now I know Andy has plans to have a family of his own. That's something I probably should have gotten around to telling him before now. It's been a few weeks, after all.

The only thing was, how exactly was one supposed to drop that into casual conversation?

'Oh, hi, love. Just so you know, your best friend, my sister, is dead, but she had a kid before she died, and I'm the stand-in daddy. Surprise!'

Yeah, that shit isn't going to fly. I know the longer I leave it, the worse it's going to be, and the more severe Andy's reaction is going to be. How much longer am I going to wait before I tell him the truth?

There's nothing else for it. It has to be this weekend.

Chapter Seventeen
Andy

I GRIN when I open my front door mid-morning and Chris is standing on the doorstep. It's been almost two weeks since I've seen him, and it was starting to feel like forever.

"Hello, you." He leans in and kisses me softly.

"Hi," I say in an almost whisper and step aside to allow him to come in. "Would you like a tour?" I ask as he stands in my hallway.

He nods. "I'd love one."

The house isn't huge. It's a four-bedroom house in a quiet end of the town. It's a family home, if I'm honest. It's my fresh start, and it seemed like the place I could have the future I wanted in. The kids, pets, maybe a partner in it with me. That was the plan anyway.

"And this is my room." I smile, opening the door to the master bedroom. His hands slip around my waist, and he pulls himself in against my back. His mouth finds my neck, and he nibbles gently at my skin before whispering in my ear, "I look forward to having you naked in here later."

I close my eyes and let his words wash over me. I've missed this man so much over the last twenty years. More than I ever wanted to admit to myself. He had always crossed my mind, but I never realised until I saw him again just how much I had always remained connected to him, despite everything.

He takes me by the hand and pulls me around to face him. "Are you okay?"

Damn him and his ability to know where my mind is.

I nod. I am okay. He's here with me, and somehow, that instantly fills something that was missing, even when I didn't know it was.

"Was this where you lived with Graham?" he asks, and I know he's assuming there's a subtle weirdness about the fact that I'm about to bring a man into what used to be my marital bedroom.

"No. I've only lived in Hatch Warren for the last two years almost. I bought this place after the divorce. It just felt right for where I wanted my life to head."

He nods.

"We lived in Southampton. He still does." I let my head fall forward a little in an attempt to hide from him. It feels strange to be talking about my marriage with my first love and who, in a convoluted way, is the reason for me having that marriage in the first place.

Chris places a finger under my chin, lifts my face to his, and gently kisses my lips. Just like that, my anxiety is lifted. He always did have that skill, even when we were kids.

"So, are you going to show me the rest of the house?" he asks.

I nod, take his hand, and lead him back to the kitchen.

Chapter Eighteen
Andy

Chris and I are sitting in my living room, having a coffee and a chat after getting back from a nice lunch in The Hatch on the other side of Basingstoke, when my phone rings. I glance at the screen and see Lucy, my surrogate, is calling me.

"Sorry, I need to answer this," I say.

I answer with a hello and head into the kitchen for a bit of privacy.

"You all right, lovely?" My stomach knots instantly at what might be coming. This isn't the first call like this I've had from Lucy after a trip to the clinic, but if this one goes like all the others, I'll have to rethink my plan for a family a little.

"I thought I would give you a call and update you on everything."

She didn't say she was okay, and instantly, I prepare myself for the worst. The knots grow and my heart hammers in my chest.

"I've been feeling a bit off the last few days, so I asked Paul to get me a test."

Paul is Lucy's wonderful other half. He has been so supportive of her and me throughout this whole process.

"Okay." There are too many thoughts racing through my head right now to say anything other than a basic acknowledgement that she's speaking to me.

"Are you sitting down?"

"Why? Oh, God. It was negative again, wasn't it?"

"Oh, sweetheart. I think you might need to. The test was positive. I'm pregnant. You're going to be a daddy! It worked!"

All the words I have ever known have left my brain, and I stand with the phone just about still against my ear and say nothing.

"Andy? Andy? Are you still there? Did you hear me? I said I'm pregnant, and you're going to be a daddy!"

For a split second, the fog lifts, and I reply, "I'm here. I'm here, I'm just... Wow."

Lucy laughs. In the background, I can hear Paul telling her to tell me he had the same reaction when he found out she was pregnant with their first. "It's just shock, my love. It will wear off. You go and take it all in, and I'll call you back tomorrow."

"Okay."

"Bye, love!"

"Bye." Another moment of clarity flickers over me. "Oh, Lucy?" I catch her just before she hangs up. "Thank you so, so much for this."

"You're very welcome. Talk soon!"

I say goodbye again and hang up the phone. I stand in the kitchen for a moment and wait for my legs to not feel like jelly, for my heart to stop pounding, and for my hands to stop shaking because the adrenaline has kicked in.

In a blind daze, I make it back into the living room. Chris takes one look at me and panics.

"Are you okay?" he asks, his face flashing with concern.

"Yeah." I nod.

He stands, taking me by the hand, and leads me back to the sofa. "Jesus, Andy. Are you sure? You look as white as a bloody sheet."

"I just had some good news."

"*Good* news? If this is how you react to good news, I'm not sure I want to see how you react to bad news."

My knees give way, and I flop into the chair beside him. "There's something I need to tell you. Something I hadn't mentioned because I didn't know what was going to happen with us, and if what *has* happened is even going to work because it hasn't before, and now it has, and I... um, well, I need to tell you."

Chris takes my hand in his. "Andy, you're not making any sense. What's happened? What do you need to tell me?"

I take a deep breath and the floodgates open. I had told him the reason Graham and I finally divorced was over children. That I wanted them and he didn't. But I hadn't told him that I planned to actually go ahead with it. That I already had those plans well in motion.

"Not long after I moved in here, I started to look for a surrogate. After a few false starts, I found Lucy. I sank the last of my savings into IVF treatment, and the first two attempts failed. The third attempt was my last shot. After that, I would have to think about how I wanted my family to happen. Would I want to go into debt for a child that was biologically mine but might never happen or go down the path of adoption?" I laugh because it seems so silly now I know what I do. "Turns out, um, well... Lucy's pregnant. It worked. I'm going to be a dad."

"Wow!" is all he says as the shock hits him.

"I know, it's a lot. I have no idea what's going to happen with you and me, and now I'm making it even more complicated because I'm going to be a dad."

He pulls me towards him and grins at me. "Andy, you are going to make an amazing dad. I mean, man, it's hard fucking work with a baby, but you're going to be fantastic."

Somehow, in the madness of the moment, my brain latches onto the one part of that comment that makes me overthink. "You sound like you speak from experience in parenting."

"I do, kinda."

I feel like I've been slapped in the face. "You have a baby?" I ask, and I can feel panic and anger flooding through my system.

He nods. "Andy, it's not what you're thinking."

"You have a baby, and you didn't think to tell me about this? Are you married?" The second those words leave my mouth, I start into a downward spiral. "Oh. My. God. You slept with me in that hotel and you're already with someone and have a baby with them." My voice gets loud enough to snap him out of his total inability to see how much of a big deal this is.

"Wait, Andy. It's not..."

I don't let him finish. I'm already on my feet, stomping to my living room door. "Not what I think, Chris? No, it never fucking is with you, is it?"

He gets up to follow me, to try to take me by the hand, but I can't let him touch me for fear of breaking down. I refuse to do that in front of him again.

"You're not listening to me!"

I turn on my heel and stare at him, my fists balled by my sides. The notion that, yet again, the same man as before is about to mess my world up all over again enrages me.

"I'm not listening? Oh, please, do tell me about the child you have with someone else that you failed to fucking mention and are only bringing up now when you have to. Once again, you've hidden things from me. What would have happened this time, Chris? Were you going to just disappear and go back to playing happy families with your partner and child?"

"It's not fucking like that." His raised voice startles me, and I stop dead, staring at him. "She's not mine. She's Zoe's, but I'm her guardian."

That makes no sense to me. Why would Zoe have abandoned her daughter? That's not the girl I was friends with at all.

"Zoe abandoned her child? Well, she wasn't like that when I knew her."

He sighs, and an emotion I'm not sure I can place washes over him.

"I should have told you this sooner too. Zoe died, Andy. Just six months ago."

The air leaves my lungs, and I want to crumble into a heap on the floor. "What? No. No, she can't have."

His shoulders sag, and his gaze drops to the floor, his eyes sparkling with tears. "I wish she hadn't. More than you know. But she's gone." He reaches into his pocket and hands me a white envelope. "She left this for you. Uh, it's why I tried to contact you on Facebook. To see about delivering this to you."

Snatching the thick envelope from his hand, I stare at it, noticing Zoe's handwriting on the front of it. "What's this?"

"It's a letter she wrote to you. She wrote one for me too,

and some for Hannah for all her milestones. I'm going to take a guess and say it's pretty emotional, cheeky, and utterly like Zoe. Mine was."

I can't take my eyes off Zoe's writing. "You know what, this is all too much to take in. You need to get the fuck out of my house," I demand, walking towards my front door.

"Andy. Stop," he pleads.

I can't stand to think about any of this for one more minute, and I pull him towards the open door. "No, you stop. You can't keep not telling me things and then dropping them on me and watching them explode like a fucking hand grenade. I'm not doing this anymore."

I shove him hard, and he stumbles over the threshold. "We need to talk about this," he says, glancing down towards the letter still in my hand.

"No! Get the fuck away from me, Chris. I don't need this. I don't need to be lied to and kept in the dark all over again." I slam the door in his face and don't let him get another word in.

"Andy!" he shouts through the letterbox.

"Just fuck off. I mean it," I tell him from the other side of the door, barely holding on to my emotions.

"Okay! Okay! I'm going."

I stand there, watching him get into his car and pull out of my driveway, and quite possibly out of my life yet again.

Chapter Nineteen
Andy

I've been driving around aimlessly for hours when I finally realise where I've come to. I've not been here in years, and it seems weird that on autopilot, it's the one place I've headed for. I park the car in West Beach car park, and I get out and walk out onto the pebble beach at the bottom of Hayling Island.

Chris brought me here once, a long time ago. This was the place where he told me we would always be together. This is the place where he told me we would get married and have children together. This is the place where he gave me a promise ring and told me he would marry me someday, as soon as he thought we were ready.

Being ready never came.

And now, here I am, standing on the same beach with a slightly different gift he's given me. I pull the envelope from my pocket and sit on the stones, watching the waves lap against the shoreline.

All the air in my lungs comes out in one long exhale, and as I suck in the fresh sea air, I open Zoe's letter.

My dearest Andy,

I have to say, cancer really is a cunt. I always thought you and I would eventually make friends again, but it's starting to look like I won't make it that far.

I owe you a huge apology for two things. The first is that I never should have kept the secret of Chris's intention to join the Navy from you. I know we were best friends, but I had this silly loyalty to him because he's my brother, and it was wrong. I was wrong. Because let's face it, it's Chris, and he's a silly twat who has a nasty habit of fucking things up. And he really did fuck it up by walking away from you. You were the best bloody thing that ever happened to him, and I should have told you so you could have tried to talk some sense into him too because Christ knows he just ignored his kid sister.

I hope one day you can forgive him. I know that's not a small thing to ask, but lately, I've been thinking a lot about forgiveness. Mostly, I've had to learn to forgive myself for leaving my little girl behind. That's not what she needs to feel from me as she grows inside me and in her first months in the world, really, is it? Her mum being all bitter at how this has all turned out.

The second thing I need to apologise for is telling Chris you were getting married. It wasn't my place. It split up our friendship, and that was worth so much to me that I shouldn't have betrayed it the way I did. I guess I just thought it was my last chance to fix the thing I shouldn't have let happen in the first place. But I regret not having been your friend in the last seventeen years, and I hope you'll forgive me for it. I don't mean that in a 'pity the poor old dying friend' kind of way. I mean that in the hand on heart, I fucked up and should have put it right years ago kind of way.

Cancer might have stolen things from me, but that isn't going to stop me from dispensing some truths and some sneaky mischief now.

The truths first. That man has never stopped loving you. There's been a boyfriend here or there, but they never get serious, and they never fill him with the same joy being with you did.

I was sorry to hear you got divorced. A friend of mine is a friend of Graham's, and they mentioned it in passing. I really hoped you would be happy despite everything that happened and would get everything in life you wanted. But I guess, for now, that hasn't happened.

So, this is my mischief. I've left it to Chris to find you and deliver this. I could easily have left it to Mum, along with the others, but this one had to come through him because, well, it's my last chance. How else can I put you into each other's paths again and see if fate can stop pissing around so you guys can have your happily ever after?

You both deserve happiness, Andy, because there isn't nearly enough of it in the world. I should be happy and looking forward to the birth of my first baby, and instead, here I am, every kick tinged with sadness because I'm not going to be here to see her grow up. I won't see her take her first steps, or blow out the candles on her birthday cakes, or the look on her face when Santa's been. And she's never going to remember how much I loved her or have me hug her and kiss her goodnight.

And I know it's a bit bloody rich that after seventeen years, I'm here dispensing the pearls of wisdom, but looking at death gives you an insane amount of clarity.

Say the things you should have said. Do the things you should have done. And if you ever get a shot to be happy, no matter how or when it happens, grab it, my friend. With both hands, and never let it go.

All my love,

Zoe xo

The tears freefall down my face by the time I get to the end of her letter. Everything that's happened, everything I've been holding in up until this point bubbles over, and I fall apart on the deserted beach as the light starts to fade.

Chapter Twenty
Chris

I'm in shock. I can't get my head around what the fuck just happened. I drive out of Basingstoke and head down the A339, feeling like a zombie.

I had it all planned out how this would go. I was going to sit him down and explain. I was going to hand over the letter and give him the time he needed to digest everything.

Until he talked about how he was going to have a baby. My mouth engaged without my brain, and the whole world caved in.

I fucked it up. *Again.*

As the miles towards Petersfield pass, I can't believe I said what I did, and that it went how it did. I keep replaying it over and over in my mind, and I can't fathom what the hell happened. I need to fix it, and I don't know how.

My mum is going to kill me when I tell her. It's at times like this I wish my sister was still here. She'd have known what to tell me.

I need to make sure Andy understands just how much he means to me, and that I had planned to tell him this weekend, no matter what. It's just that the wheels came off that particular wagon.

I think about what Zoe would have said about all of this. Wherever she is now, I know she'll be laughing at me for making such a mess of it all. I think about stopping off at Kingston Cemetery before heading to my mum's to collect the baby.

I stand over the plot where Zoe was laid to rest just a few months ago.

"Hello, Zoe. Sorry it's been a while since I've been here." I pause and nod to a little old lady as she passes by with a bunch of flowers. "Christ, you would kick my arse if you were here and laughing in my stupid face. I have well and truly fucked this one up all over again, sis."

I squat down to fix the flowers my mum had left on the grave the last time she was here.

"I've been seeing Andy again," I tell her. "It's been about three weeks so far, and I know I should have told him sooner that this is where you are now, and all about Hannah, but I couldn't find the right time to tell him. And then, today, while I was there, he found out he's about to be a dad, and what did your idiot brother do? He went and blabbed that he already has a child, and now Andy thinks I'm a useless shit for lying to him all over again, just like last time."

In my head, I can hear what Zoe would have said to me at this point. She'd have told me I'm a stupid twat. She'd have told me I need to get my arse in gear and get this fixed because I've let Andy down enough.

"You always knew what to say, Zoe," I say, my eyes scanning over the writing on her headstone.

I think some more about what she would have said to me. I really should have listened more to what my kid sister told me. She'd have given me a big hug and told me she loved me but that I needed to get my shit together or she'd kick my arse because we only had one chance at life, and we needed to grab it by the fucking balls anytime we had the chance.

"I miss you. You should be here for this little girl of yours, not me." I stand and stay there, saying nothing for a minute with my head down.

"Are you okay, love?" The little old lady is back and looking at me sympathetically.

I wave to her and smile. "Fine, thanks. Just having a chat with my sister," I say, nodding toward the grave.

She nods. "I talk to my Sydney all the time. Never talks back, the cheeky bugger. We still know what they would say to us, though, don't we?"

Smiling back at her, I nod. "That we do."

"Whatever she's telling you, you look like you need to be listening."

I laugh, and she gives me a wink as she walks off. "Take care, love."

"You too." I smirk and glance back at Zoe's grave. "You did that, didn't you?" I whisper. "I'll sort it. I promise."

———

Three hours later, my mother has finally stopped telling me what a moron I've been. She tells me I need to get on the phone to Andy right this minute and make it right. I nod and pull my phone from my pocket and nod towards the garden.

I scroll to Andy's number and hit call.

It rings and rings, and then it goes to voicemail.

I hit cancel and try to call him again. This time, it goes straight to voicemail.

My phone chirps with a text. It's from Andy.

Am driving.

I sigh, shove my phone back in my pocket, and head back inside to gather Hannah's stuff and head home.

I've changed Hannah, and I'm sitting on the rocking chair in her nursery, giving her a feed before putting her down for the night.

"Your uncle is a big ninny," I whisper to her. "The only advice I will ever have for you when you're older, my beautiful girl, is that if your uncle would do it, it's the wrong choice."

She grins at me with a little burp, and I snuggle her against me.

"Your mummy would know how to fix this. I really miss her, little one."

I kiss Hannah's forehead and watch as she falls asleep in my arms.

Chapter Twenty-One
Andy

I HADN'T HEARD anything from Chris since I texted him to say I was driving nine days ago. *Yes, I was counting.* I don't know what I was expecting. I think I just hoped there would be something instead of nothing. I've been thinking non-stop about Zoe's letter. I've thought about how he looked when I kicked him out. I've been trying to figure out what I want to do next.

I've taken some time off work. Mostly because Fiona has been getting on my last nerve, but a little because I really needed time to myself to reflect on what's going to happen and how I'm going to cope with it all.

Has he explained himself yet? My sister texts.

No. I reply.

My phone rings, and it's Laura.
"The thing you have to ask yourself, Andy, is what the fuck are you going to do now?"
I sigh. I should have known when my sister moves from

texting me to calling me that this will be how the conversation will go.

"I dunno, Lala. I just don't know."

"So, you're chicken shit. Is that what you're telling me?"

I roll my eyes. "Jesus, Laura. That's some lovely language there. I'm not sure I want to talk about this anymore. I'm not sure I have any of the answers you think I should," I say, hoping to deflect her from further comments on the subject.

I know what Laura thinks I should do. I'm pretty sure she's thinking the same things as Zoe, and how life is short.

"Hmmm." I don't need to see my sister's face to know that I would be getting that look that's reserved for when she thinks I'm talking out of my backside but doesn't want to call me on it verbally. She seems to have forgotten that stopped working on me when I hit seventeen, around the same time Chris disappeared on me the first time.

"Look, I've got a killer headache, and I need to go and lie down in a dark, quiet room." I lie just to get off the phone.

"Right." Yeah, she's not buying that for a second.

"Love you," I say.

She sighs in defeat. "Love you too."

Without overthinking it to death and while my phone is still in my hand, I tap on Chris's name and type out a quick message.

I think we need to talk about all of this. Can you come over?

Three little dots drum on the screen, and then his reply appears.

I'll be there in about forty-five minutes.

I busy myself around the house, trying not to dwell on what's about to be said or happen.

Chapter Twenty-Two
Andy

THERE'S one thing I learned from my marriage with Graham. Honesty is key. If I'm going to listen to Zoe's advice and attempt to grab happiness while I can, I need to be honest with Chris and clear the air first. We have to talk about why his dishonesty pissed me off. He needs to know that if we are to move forward together, he needs to work on that, or this is never going to work.

He walks into my house like a man waiting to hear if he's been sentenced to death. I haven't told him what Zoe said yet. I haven't said anything other than we need to talk.

"So, you wanted to talk?"

I gesture for him to sit on the far end of the sofa. "I'm not happy with what happened here last time, Chris."

He nods, sinking into the chair, the empty cushion between us feeling like a chasm. "I can understand that."

"Can you? Because the way I see it, I don't know if I can trust you. You repeatedly keep things from me, and I don't know what I'm meant to do with that."

His head hangs forward. "I don't know what to say to that."

"You lied to me, Chris. Again!" I'm seething with a rage I didn't know I had within me.

"I meant to tell you. I wanted to, but the right time never presented itself. So it ended up with me not telling you, and I'm sorry for that."

His words mean nothing and have zero impact on my wounded state. All I can see is his lack of honesty.

"A lie by omission is still a fucking lie!" Some part of me knows that he's well aware that knows that, but my anger takes over. He watches from the sofa, as I rise and start to pace up and down the living room like a caged tiger. "You don't get it, do you?" I bark.

"No, I do…"

"You don't." I cut him off. "I trusted you. You were my everything, and you left me high and fucking dry without a word."

"I'm sor-"

My hand shoots up in a gesture to silence him. "No. You will hear this, and you'll listen without interruption. You once accused me of picking Graham because he was the safe option, and you know what? You were right. He was safe because I loved him and he loved me, because he talked to me about his feelings, even the bad ones, and he wanted to plan an actual future with me and not just run away from it."

Chris stares at me, and I know the thoughts in his head without him saying a word. I know he wants to defend himself, and I also know he's holding back, just to let me finally get it all out.

"Yes, I know we divorced because we didn't want the

same things in the end, but at least he fucking stuck around and tried."

His shoulders sag.

"Now, when I'm trying to learn to trust you again, you pull this shit. You have a nasty habit of telling me *nothing*, and then wondering what happened when it all explodes in your fucking face." My feet stop moving and I stand staring at him. "These aren't small things. They are monumental things." My voice softens, admiring his self-control to not try to argue with me, to fight his point, and to just let me vent. "A child and your sister's death are high things, my darlin', and you saw fit to share none of them. Do you not understand that it constantly leaves me wondering what else you're not telling me?" I stare at him, willing an answer out of him.

"I do understand, Andy. But I fucked up all those years ago, and I needed to make sure that I didn't do that again. At first, I didn't know how to tell you all those things. That first night definitely wasn't the time. And then it was just how to tell you rather than when. Your best friend, that you'd fallen out with because of me, had died before you'd been reconnected again." He shrugs. "With the baby, well, I couldn't explain her without explaining Zoe, and then too much time had passed without me mentioning it, and it got bigger and bigger. Just like telling you I was going to join the Navy."

Had he planned to tell me about leaving? I glare at him all the more.

"You had all these amazing plans, Andy. You were going to go to university to study art. You were going to travel and get inspiration. You were going to do your thing and be amazing. And I know those were *our* plans, and we talked about doing them together. But I still felt like I had no purpose, no future mapped out for me as a person away from you and me, and absolutely shit all to offer you."

Anger bubbles up, and I pace again. Did he really not understand?

"Why are you angry about that?"

My mouth falls open, and my movements pause. "Are you really that fucking stupid? What part of us making all those plans together translated to you *not* being there with me? That the reason I was so hopeful and full of fun and wonder was that everything was going to be done with the love of my life right by my side for all of it."

Regret, sadness, and the penny dropping flashes over his features, and he looks like he wants the ground to open up and swallow him. This time, my feet move to keep myself from going to him and comforting him. He needs to understand this. To feel it as I did.

"I did none of those things. It felt wrong to do any of that without you there with me. And if you had bothered to talk to me about anything you were feeling back then, we might have been able to get through it. At the very least, you could have talked over your feelings, and I would have understood why you felt the need to go and make something of yourself, I would have waited. I wouldn't have felt so utterly destroyed."

He looks up at me and raises an eyebrow. "You married someone else, Andy. That doesn't really scream of destruction."

"Fuck you, Chris Cooper."

He recoils at the harshness of my tone.

"You don't get to sit there and have the nerve to make out that because I made a life for myself after you left me that your departure didn't leave me desolate. My whole world crumbled to nothing. All my plans, dreams, and hopes died when you left, and I spent months mourning the what-could-have-beens. Your sister got me through it. Your sister is the one who told me you were a prick and talked me around from giving up on love or anything else. I did what I could with the life I was left with. You *never* get to shit on me for that. Ever."

He stands at my words and moves towards me. "I'm jealous, and I'm sorry my words made you feel like your feelings were unjustified. They are perfectly valid. I was wrong, and I *am* sorry."

He takes my hands in his.

"And you're also right that I was a prick. Zoe always said I had been for not telling you. Fear drove me then, and fear drove me this time too. I was scared, Andy. Scared that, back then, you would have talked me out of it and that you'd have hated me for being someone who just tagged along with your dreams without any fulfilment of my own, and that eventually, you would find someone who was a better fit for you, and then where would I have been?"

"In the same place you left me when you joined the Navy."

He sighs. "Andy, you don't know how lucky you've been in life. I have lived with the regret of leaving you back then for my whole life. You moved on, you got married. You built a home, a relationship. You planned a future, and you built a business."

"So did you."

I shake my head. "I threw myself into the only thing I had left, and I promised myself that if I ever had the chance to hold on to the happiness I once had with you again, I would never let it go. I was wrong, and you will never know how limiting that regret can be. I deserve you hating me for what I did. I can take your anger. But what I can't take is you thinking I'm just out to keep fucking you over, because I'm not. I'm just a human who makes mistakes. Ones I wish to fuck weren't as big as they seem to keep being."

His confession makes my heart skip a beat. With everything that's happened, I never thought of it in those terms; of how it would seem to him looking in from the outside of my life after he left. "I'm sorry too."

He closes his eyes at my words and pulls my hands to his lips, kissing my knuckles. "How can I fix this?"

"Honestly, I don't know. I'm not sure you can."

"There has to be a way forward with this, Andy. I'm not willing to lose you again. I was stupid enough to let that happen once, but twice? No. I refuse to let it happen again."

Something within me admires his determination, even if I'm not sure he's worthy of my trust.

"Do you want to know what Zoe told me?" I ask.

He looks at me with a sadness I don't think I've ever seen on him since the day I slapped his face before my nuptials with Graham.

"Only if you're sure you want to tell me."

"She apologised. For ruining the friendship we had, for not telling me you were joining the Navy, and for telling you I was getting married. She told me that cancer was shit for all the things it was robbing from her, but that that gave her a unique perspective on things."

He nods with a soft smile. "Sounds like her."

"She tried to set this up," I say, wagging my finger back and forth between us.

"What?" He shakes his head, not understanding what I mean.

"The letter. She was scheming. She thought once we saw each other again, things would happen. She knew I was divorced, and she gave me some advice, and she told me the letter was her way of getting you and me in the same place at the same time."

A snort escapes from his lips, and he shakes his head with a smile. "She always was a conniving little cow." He laughs.

"She was right about something, though."

Chris looks at me with a furrowed brow.

"Apparently, all it *did* take was for us to be in the same room at the same time."

The filthy smirk I love creeps over his features as he thinks about what happened between us that night in the hotel. He raises an eyebrow suggestively. "She might have had a point on that one."

"She left me with a lot to think about after you left. About life, love, happiness, and she has me thinking about forgiveness."

When our eyes connect, I'm greeted with a sparkle of hope shining in his.

"If this is ever going to work between us, Chris, I need two things to happen. I need to forgive you for what happened all those years ago, but I also need you to learn from it. To understand where you made mistakes and the damage they did and endeavour to never do that again."

"Can you forgive me?"

I feel like I'm looking at a lost puppy with big sad eyes, begging me to take it home with me. I nod.

"Then I can learn. I've thought about it a lot in the last twenty years, and in the last few weeks."

I smile at him. My heart flips at the thought of this actually happening. Chris stands and moves towards where I've been pacing this whole time. His arms wrap around me, and he pulls me into one of his soul-soothing, all-encompassing hugs.

The feeling I had before is back. This is home, and this is where I want to stay.

Chapter Twenty-Three
Chris

THINGS HAVE BEEN MOVING ALONG in the last week since Andy and I had our heart-to-heart about the mistakes of the past and the possibilities for the future. I've never been more grateful to have him back in my life, but today is going to be a big deal for us. I'm heading back to Basingstoke to see him, but this time, I'm going to have Hannah with me. Today, she gets to finally meet the man who I hope will be her Uncle Andy one day. I just hope it will all work out as I want it to.

I pull into Andy's drive and sit there for a moment, rubbing my hands over the steering wheel, trying to quell the nervous knot in my stomach.

Hannah babbles in the back seat, and I smile. "Okay, boss. I know you don't like it when the car stops moving."

I hop out of the driver's seat, grab her nappy bag from the boot, open the back door, and spin her car seat towards me. I scoop her small form out of the car and smile at her.

"All ready to meet Uncle Chris's favourite person in the whole wide world?"

She grins at me and babbles against my shoulder as I carry her to Andy's front door.

I knock, and almost instantly, Andy answers with a smile.

"Hi."

"Hi. And hello, little gorgeous one," he coos in Hannah's direction, smoothing out her dress. She grins at him a little and then nuzzles herself into my shoulder.

"God, she is the spitting image of Zoe," he says as he backs away from the door to let us come inside.

"She is, isn't she? She's like a mini-Zoe, and it's funny because she's already starting to be like her in personality too."

Andy puts his hands out to my niece, offering to take her from me, and after an initial eye of suspicion, she surprises me by reaching out to him and letting him hold her.

"Why? Is she a cheeky one?" He grins, bouncing her up and down tucked against him.

She gives him a grin that would have me believe she understood exactly what she was being accused of, and then chomped on his t-shirt with a little shriek of mischief.

I've never seen Hannah take to anyone this quickly before. I can't help but wonder if it's a sign this is all going how it's meant to be, and this is the way things will progress for us.

"What's wrong?" Andy asks, his voice still sing-songing so as not to worry the baby.

"Nothing." I snap out of my little daze of shock and universe pondering, pat Hannah on the back, making a face at her, and then continue, "She's usually a little shy thing who never makes friends with someone as quickly as she has with you."

"Are you a good judge of character, just like your mum?" Andy coos at her. Her little face lights up with yet another smile.

"She must be," I agree.

"Let's get you in and more comfortable, shall we?" Andy nods towards the living room, and I follow his lead.

The hours spent talking about Hannah and Zoe fly past, and eventually, she's asleep, and Andy and I can grab some lunch.

"You're a natural, you know?"

He looks at me with a grin. "Do you really think so?"

I nod. "I know so. That baby doesn't like strangers, and yet she let you hold her instantly. Kids know."

He hands me a cup of coffee and smiles. "Zoe would have made an amazing mum."

I take a long sip from my mug and think about that. He's right, of course. My sister would have made an amazing mum, but I can't help but think she was anyway, despite the short amount of time she was granted with her baby. From the second that Zoe found out she was pregnant from a drunken fumble with a stranger, she had loved the life inside her with all of her being. She had thought of almost everything. She left letters for almost every conceivable event in Hannah's future life. A letter for her wedding, for the birth of her first baby, if she came out. There are letters for every single birthday until she's eighteen, and a card for every year until she's twenty-one, and then for all the big birthdays, the ones with zeros. There are a few gifts too. My mum has them all tucked away for now, but she told me about them. None of us knew how much planning for her child's future my sister was putting in. A future fate would cruelly deny her, and that she was inserting herself into anyway, in any damn way she could.

Andy and I had chatted about it while we played with Hannah on her mat on the living room floor. I'd told him all the amazing things my sister had sorted out, and she'd done it all while she had been pregnant. She was an exceptional human being.

His hand on mine brings me back to reality.

"Sorry," I mumble, my voice stuttering, caught in the emotions of grief.

He squeezes my hand a little tighter. "I can't even begin to imagine how hard this has been for you, Chris. To lose your sister is one thing, but to then have to deal with being a first-time parent to a baby while you're still grieving and looking at that beautiful little face and being reminded still of that loss."

I lace my fingers through his and return the support right back to him. He gets it more than anyone else other than my mum, and yet it's totally different for her too. She buried her child, a pain I don't know that I could ever survive when I look at Hannah and think of what it must be like for Mum.

"I didn't realise it would be this hard," I admit. It's the first time I've ever been able to say those words out loud. It *is* hard. I miss my sister every single day, and yet I have to be strong and carry on because I have an entire little person relying on me keeping my shit together. It's exhausting, and I'm not ashamed to say that I have times when I finally get Hannah down for the night and I cry in the darkness of the bathroom, overwhelmed by everything.

"I'm here anytime you need to talk, or rant, or..." He pauses, and I know right then that he knows everything I'm not saying, "anything at all."

I have no reply other than to move from where I'm sitting until I'm standing right in front of him, placing my lips on his, thanking him for his understanding, his support, and the unspoken promise of more, of being there into the future with me.

He wraps his arms around me and pulls me tight against him. There's a fire in his kiss and his embrace, and if Hannah wasn't with me, I would be taking him to bed, but it doesn't feel quite right to be getting up to anything too naughty with him the very first time that I have my niece at his house.

"We'll have to pick this up later, when Hannah is with her Nanna." He breathes against my lips, his forehead touching mine.

I smile warmly. This man is having a day where everything he does is impressing me with his kindness and understanding. Even this. It gives me hope for the future that until that moment I didn't even realise I had been missing. His caring, his affection, his baby entertaining skills, it's all just the missing piece of a puzzle I hadn't yet started to look for.

Sure, when it comes to caring for Hannah, I always have my mum for encouragement, and I know she loves and supports me, but this is different. I didn't know how much I wanted to share all of this with someone until there were little glimmers of what it might be like by being around Andy. For the first time since his wedding all those years ago, I find myself thinking about the possibilities of such things. Love, companionship, passion, all of it, right there in front of me, in one Andy-shaped package.

Suddenly, I see my future mapped out before me, and I know how I want it to be. With Andy, just as it should have been all those years ago. Just how I'm determined to make it happen now.

Chapter Twenty-Four
Andy

Nervous doesn't even begin to cover what I feel right now. I'm pacing the corridor of the maternity hospital in Southampton, waiting to see what's going on with Lucy's pregnancy.

She's twenty weeks along now, and she's been invited in for an ultrasound to check everything is okay and there are no abnormalities. She has been lovely, and Chris is allowed to come in with me.

"Hello, Dads." The technician smiles when she calls us into the room.

"Oh, I'm not..." Chris shakes his head. "Just the dad's partner."

My heart skips when he says it because it's the first time he's put a proper label on what's going on between us. I mean, sure, things have been getting more and more cemented. He stays over at mine a lot. Hannah comes with him a lot, and we do things in what feels like a family unit. But I never quite let myself believe it's actually as serious as he's willing to tell strangers it is right now. Yes, he's here with me at the scan, but I never allowed myself to read anything other than support into that. Until now.

"Hi, guys." Lucy beams from the table, where her round belly is exposed and ready. She's had the initial assessments done without us, Paul sitting in with her and making sure all is okay. And now it's our turn to see everything in black and white, and hopefully 3D.

"So, as I was telling Lucy, everything is looking amazingly well. Everything is developing as it should be." I squeeze Lucy's hand with one of mine, and Chris's with the other. "There was something we noticed that you will need to have a look at."

My heart sinks, panic takes over, and I stare at the technician, her words registering but not really making it all the way into my brain for proper processing. I'm stuck on there being a problem.

"What's wrong?" My mouth is so dry already that the words almost don't come out.

Lucy rubs my arm. "No, no! It's nothing like that, darlin'. It's all perfectly healthy and happy in there," she reassures me.

The technician smiles at Chris and then me before interjecting, "It's just a little crowded."

Something flickers on the screen for us to look at. Chris seems to understand what he's looking at almost instantly, and a huge grin erupts across his face.

I stare at the screen. The information is there for me to take in, but my brain can't understand it quickly enough. Chris puts his arm around my shoulder and kisses my cheek. "There's two there, right?" he confirms with the technician.

Lucy and the woman with the baby viewing wand nod.

"Two?" I look at him.

"Babies, Andy. You said three were implanted, right? Looks like two of them wanted to stay and say hello."

I shook my head. "But there have been other scans. No one said this before?" I had to be dreaming.

The technician highlighted each baby on the screen. "It can be common when they're both lying the same way, one toward the front and one towards the back, to miss it. Especially with the standard early pregnancy scans. This one is a bit bigger and clearer, and we check everything from almost every angle, and they don't get to hide out behind their sibling anymore."

"Two." I nod my head. I have no other response to give.

"Can you tell if they are boys or girls yet?" Chris asks, turning to me. "You wanted to know, right?"

Again, the only reply I have is a movement of confirmation with my head.

The technician moves the wand over Lucy's belly, and the images on the screen—the babies—move. She stops over one and points to an area on the monitor.

"That is baby A, and that right there is a penis."

She moves the wand around again, and another little form becomes clear on the screen. "And that's baby B, and that looks very much like a girl."

A boy and a girl. I have no idea what the hell I'm meant to do with two babies. Shell shocked by the information is an understatement.

Chris smiles at the technician on my behalf. "Thank you so much. Andy has wanted this for so long. I think he's just completely overwhelmed right now."

She smiles warmly. "He's not the first, and he'll not be the last, I'm sure." She reaches down to the printer under the machine and tears off a little strip of images. "Here you go." She hands them to me. "Babies' first pictures."

She hands Lucy a strip of blue paper towel and helps her to clean the goop off her stomach that was used to get a good image of the babies. Lucy adjusts her leggings and her top back over her belly and gets to her feet. Her arms are tight around me before I can even offer her a hand of assistance.

"Congratulations, Andy. I'm so happy this has worked out for you." She smiles at Chris and squeezes his hand. "I think he might need a brandy." She chuckles, and we all leave the ultrasound suite together.

Chapter Twenty-Five
Andy

IT'S BEEN a few days since the high-drama baby reveal, and I think the notion of having to care for two tiny humans might finally be starting to sink in.

It's monumental, but just as surprising to me was Chris's reaction to it all.

"You surprised me a little the other day, you know?" I begin as I flop down on my sofa beside him.

"I did?" He smiles, wrapping an arm around my shoulder.

"Yeah." I pause, trying to think of the best way to express what I'm feeling. Trying to fight the pounding of my heart and the sudden dryness of my mouth. "First you said you were my partner, and then you took the news about it being twins completely in your stride, and you were just *there* for me."

"You daft bugger. I love you. Of course I'm going to support you. Though there's going to need to be a rethink on the nursery now you're kitting it out for two." He chuckles. "But I'm here to help."

"You are, aren't you." I'm not really asking him. I'm

merely acknowledging what I'm finally realising and believing right through to my soul. "Do you want to be their dad too?" I blurt out.

The thought has been swimming around in my head since he corrected the technician to say he wasn't the dad, just the partner. It felt wrong that he would deny himself that. It tugged at my heart and felt like a giant mis-step to have him on the outside of all this when he felt like he had become a part of it. An important part I didn't want to do without.

He looks at me in stunned silence, blinking at me, and I instantly overthink it. I've said too much. He hasn't thought about this at all. I want to backtrack. "Look..." I start.

"Yes," he interrupts.

Now it's my turn to be lost for words. "Yes?" I parrot after a moment.

"Yes, Andy. I want to be here for you and them. Forever."

I stare at him as he moves to where his jacket is draped over the back of the sofa and starts rummaging in the pockets. Once he has what he was looking for, he turns back towards me.

"I've had this for a few weeks now. As usual, I couldn't find the right time for it, but now seems like the perfect time."

I watch as everything slows down. Chris is sinking to the floor in front of me on one knee. He looks up at me, opens the box in his hand, and he smiles. I'm so lost in his actions that I almost don't hear the words when he says them.

"Andrew Reese, we've had a very long and crazy path to get to this point. But I'd really love it if you would finally do me the honour of being my husband. I know this might seem fast, but we've known each other for decades, and well, if the last year has taught me anything, it's that life is short as fuck. So, what do you say? Marry me?"

For the first time in a long time, I don't have a single hesitation or thought in my head. Instead, my heart is full, and I can think of no good reason to wait. "Yes!" I say the second he stops talking. "Yes, Chris Cooper. I would very much like to marry you."

His grin grows exponentially, and so does the twinkle in his eyes as he slides the ring up the third finger on my left hand. A second later, he's standing in front of me and his mouth is on mine. His arms are tight around me and he's kissing me like he's been starved of affection for months.

This man was genuinely terrified I would say no. The tension in his body dissipates. I can taste the relief in his mouth. From the kiss, he moves to one of his trademark all-encompassing hugs. He squeezes me tightly, and I melt into it. How right it feels. How much that feeling of home is wrapped up in this man.

He drops his arms from around me, grabs my hand, and pulls me towards the stairs.

"What are you doing?" I laugh.

He gives me a look that has goosebumps prickling over my skin. I know exactly where this is going. "I'm taking my fiancé to bed."

I grin and let him lead me upstairs.

Chapter Twenty-Six
Chris

To say Andy had just made me the happiest man alive would be a massive understatement. I don't have enough words to express how much Andy, his babies, and his acceptance of my proposal mean to me.

So, I'm going to do the only other thing I can do. I'm going to make love to the man who is going to be my husband. I've waited what feels like a lifetime for this to finally happen, and I can't believe my secret hopes and desires—and my cheeky sister's secret scheming—has actually come to fruition.

Andy is going to be Mr Andy Cooper. It's a presumption, but it's one based on the conversations we had about it when we were teenagers. One day, we would get married, and one day, he was going to be the other Mr Cooper in the relationship.

As we cross the threshold of his bedroom, I don't waste a second. I step into his space and seize his mouth with my own. I lick over his lips, begging him to let my tongue in, and when he finally does, I moan against his mouth and take my fill of him, rolling my tongue over his.

Andy grabs the hem of my t-shirt and yanks it over my head. His hands roaming over my back, grabbing at me, pulling me hard against him. I can feel his dick through our jeans; the man is very much ready for anything I would like to do with him here. But then, so am I.

I pull his t-shirt off and use it like a strap behind his head to pull his mouth back to mine before tossing it to the floor. Andy breaks our kiss and moves his mouth over my jaw, nibbling on my earlobe, kissing along my neck, then peppering a trail of kisses and nibbles over my torso until he's sitting on the bed and I'm standing between his legs.

His eyes fall on what's directly in front of him, and he reaches for the zipper of my jeans with a smirk. Fuck, this man is my undoing, and I have never been happier. Andy watches me intently with pure wanton lust as he slips my jeans over my hips and then slides my boxers down to meet them on my thighs.

My cock is standing proud and letting him know how much he turns me on. He gives his eyebrows a cheeky raise and licks his lips before wrapping his mouth around my length and running his tongue along the underside of my cock.

"Holy fuck." I exhale, keeping my eyes on his, not wanting to break the intensity of the moment.

Andy reaches around me, grabs my arse, and pulls me towards him, not stopping until I hit the back of his throat and trigger his gag reflex. He stays there, looking up at me, and I stare down at him, willing him to move yet delighting in the feeling of his mouth and throat clasping around my cock as he tries to breathe through the retching.

I can't keep looking at the passion of his gaze for a second longer with the sensations he's serving me, and I close my eyes, let my head fall back, and growl with a slight jerk of my hips. I need him to suck me. I need him to lap his tongue over the tip of my dick and work the absolute magic I know he's capable of until I can't take it anymore.

When I look back down at him, that's exactly what he's doing. The last time I climaxed from getting a blow job, I was a teenager and still with Andy. No one else has ever been able to achieve that for me. And as much as Andy is getting me so damn close to that again, I really want to be balls deep inside him when I finally shoot my load.

He starts to work me over with his mouth. Just the right amount of pressure as he sucks, bobbing his head up and down on my prick. Then he runs his tongue along the underneath of my shaft before rolling it over the head of my cock. His mouth is wet and warm and utterly incredible. "Fuck, Andy. You're going to make me bust my fucking nut."

He smiles around my cock, and as amazing as his mouth is on me, it's not enough.

"Enough of the teasing." I growl and take a step back from him, letting my cock fall free of his mouth. "Strip."

Andy smirks at my command and slowly rises, kicking off his trainers and watching my reaction as he lingers a moment, slowly undoing his jeans and sliding them and his briefs down his legs. I waste no time in doing the same with the last of my clothing. As I step out of my underwear, the sight of Andy's sexy arse greets me as he gets on his bed on his hands and knees, inviting me to have my way with him.

I grab the lube from where it lives on the top of his dresser, smother my cock in the slippery substance, and move onto the bed right behind Andy, feeling like a predator stalking a very delicious prey.

"Move up and roll over," I say, raising an eyebrow as he

looks over his shoulder at me with the most smouldering look I have ever seen him wear.

He smiles coyly and moves to the top of the bed, resting on his back and looking up at me expectantly.

I know I should have a little more foreplay. My intention had been to make love to my new fiancé, but when he looks so amazing and ready like this, who am I to resist him?

He lifts his legs towards his waist and parts them for me. I slide my hands over his calves, the feeling of the hair skimming my fingertips. The look he's giving me fuels my hunger for him, and I can't wait a second longer. I slide the head of my cock over his arsehole, slicking it up a little from the lube before pressing it against him and waiting for his body to let me in. Moments later, it does, and I waste no time in making damn sure that my husband-to-be is utterly filled by my dick.

Chapter Twenty-Seven
Andy

Chris's look is positively predatory, and it fills me with nervous excitement. When he skims his hands over my shins and calves, my skin prickles with electricity. I haven't felt like this with someone in a very long time. Since the last time I was with Chris before he left me high and dry. I had almost forgotten how good this could feel. Almost.

The second he presses the head of his cock against my asshole, I know from the look on his face that he's not stopping until he's buried inside me. My dick twitches at the delicious anticipation of him doing just that.

"Oh, fuck. Your cock feels so good." I sigh as Chris's balls touch my buttocks. He rolls his hips, and I gasp.

"Your arse is better," he rasps and leans over to catch my mouth with his.

His movements are slow and almost lazy, but they're stirring emotions and delicious sensations within me. Chris isn't fucking me, he's making love to me in a way only he can. He makes me feel like I'm the sexiest man in the world, and with every touch, kiss, and thrust, I feel like I'm being cherished and worshipped all at once. If I'm honest, no one else has ever come close to making me feel like this.

Chris thrusts into me again and again, and the most intense slow-burn orgasm builds within me. He moves his mouth to my nipples, and I feel like it's directly wired to my dick. The sensation is thrilling. I run my hands over his short hair and moan his name as he rolls his hips again.

His worshipping of me climbs in intensity, and I can't help but wrap my legs around him and keep him where I need him the most. There's something extremely enticing about being so completely taken by a man, yet surrounded by a bubble of love where only he and I exist. It's blissful to say the least.

The tempo of Chris's hips becomes more staccato, his mouth moves from my chest, and his hand reaches between us to my cock. "Come with me."

While his voice is commanding and dominant, there's a softness in his eyes that's pleading with me. Everything he has been doing has been leading me to this point, and with his hand on my dick, I'm not going to last long at all.

I can tell from the look on his face he isn't either. I have never wanted anything as much as I want to be in this moment with Chris. Children on the way, plans to get married, in bed making love to him. Everything is like the fairy tale I always wanted but never thought I would have.

The force of Chris's hand around the head of my cock has me quickly on the edge, and I stare into his eyes. My hand strokes his cheek, and both of us climax hard, never losing eye contact.

The intensity of the whole thing overtakes me. "I love you, Chris Cooper. Please don't ever leave me again." Tears I didn't know I had form in the corners of my eyes.

"Never, ever again," he whispers and catches my mouth with his, kissing me hard as we come down from our post-orgasmic haze.

Chapter Twenty-Eight
Chris

Four months later

WHEN I LOOK at our families gathered around for our joint housewarming, engagement, and first birthday party for Hannah, I can't help but reflect on how far Andy and I have come in a short time. Yes, it's been a long road to get here, but now we are, we're wasting no time at all in living life as fully as we can together.

We've been exceptionally lucky. My house and Andy's in Basingstoke sold so damn fast. And together, we pooled our resources and managed to get our dream forever home. Six gorgeous bedrooms, a massive new kitchen-cum-family room, and room for the family and house to grow if we need it. It's perfect, and we've worked tirelessly to get it ready in time for the twins.

Andy's sister raises her glass and nods to me. "It's about bloody time you made my brother happy and let him make an honest man out of you."

Andy rolls his eyes, and I bow in her direction, acknowledging her little dig with good humour. She's right. I shouldn't have been a prick all those years ago and should have had the balls to stick around. This time, not even the devil himself could tear me away from Andy's side.

My mum is next. "This is a beautiful home, you two, and I hope you will have very many happy years here together with your lovely family." She raises her glass, and everyone responds with cheers. Then she continues, "And, Andy, love, if he gives you any more shit, you just tell me. He's not too old to have his arse smacked."

Everyone laughs, and I'm starting to see a pattern in this evening's comments already.

Andy smiles at me and pulls him in against him. "Now, now. If anyone is to take a potshot at my soon-to-be husband, it'll be me." He gives me a cheeky wink, and I know I'm in trouble. "Two decades or so ago, this man broke my heart, and he sucked for it. But now, fate and a very dear friend worked in our favour to make sure we got the chance to fix his mistakes and put us back in each other's lives. And for that, I will be eternally grateful. Here's to righting past wrongs and creating a whole new and beautiful future together."

Andy's mum and sister reach for tissues. He has a way with words, my husband-to-be. And while they can sometimes be at my expense, I wouldn't have it any other way.

***

Three days later

I look at the clock when Andy's phone rings. Four a.m.

"Oh, Jesus," he says after a short pause. "Okay, okay. Yeah, we're on our way."

He turns to me, and I smile. "It's okay," I reassure him.

"I'll go into the guest room and wake Mum to let her know we need to go."

I get up, knock on the door of our spare room where my mum has been staying since Lucy got so close to her due date, and wake her up.

"No worries, son. You pair get going and call me as soon as anything happens. Hannah will be fine here with her nanna."

When I come back into the bedroom, I'm greeted by the sight of my partner struggling to put his socks on in a frantic state. I climb onto the bed behind him and wrap my arms around him. "Darlin', you need to breathe or you're going to pass out." I feel his body calm the tiniest fraction against mine.

"I know, it's just..."

"I know." I kiss his bare shoulder. "Just take a minute and breathe."

He leans his head back against my shoulder and closes his eyes, focussing on only taking deep breaths in and out.

"Better?" I ask after giving him a few moments to compose himself a little. He nods.

"Then let's get ready and go."

The drive from here along the M27 to Southampton's Princess Anne Hospital won't take long at this time of night.

Mum follows us down to the front door, giving us both a hug, Andy getting the bigger, tighter one.

"Good luck, love. You're going to be amazing," she reassures him.

I thank her for keeping Hannah for us, kiss her cheek, and head for the hospital where our family is set to grow.

• • •

During the journey to the hospital, Andy's knee bounces up and down in the darkness of the car. He always has a touch of restless leg when he's nervous. The tense energy is rolling off him in waves, and I know there's nothing I can do or say to take the edge off it. I'm nervous as hell myself. Hannah is only just one, and now we're about to have two more children. The prospect of three kids under two is terrifying.

I do the only thing I can at times like this. I reach out in the darkness and take his hand in mine, never happier that I picked an auto for our seven-seater family car.

"What if I fuck this all up?" he blurts out in the darkness.

"You won't."

"How do you know?"

I smile at him. "Because I know you, and I've seen you with your nieces and nephews, and I've seen you with Hannah. You are a natural dad, and you're going to be amazing with these two."

He sighs. "I hope you're right."

"I know I am."

It's just gone ten in the morning, and I'm sitting on a hospital chair with my bare-chested fiancé, who has two brand new humans lying on him. Zoe Olivia, who will be known by Olivia, and Henry Charles, named for both our fathers. He's been sitting with them like this for at least an hour now, and they're only about two hours old.

"I can't believe these are mine." He grins at me.

"You look so damn happy." I rub his arm, the one that's tucked under two tiny bums.

"You need to do this now."

"What, have a baby of my own? Jesus, do you not think we have enough on our plates already?" I laugh.

He sighs and rolls his eyes. "Your Daddy Chris is a bit silly sometimes," he whispers as he kisses their little heads. "No, you need to strip off, skin on skin with them. It's for bonding."

I stare at him. I knew he wanted me involved, but I guess in some part of my head, I just never joined the dots of what that really meant. "Oh!" I say, staring at him. "Are you sure?"

"Get your bloody t-shirt off. These are *our* babies."

I nod and fumble to pull my chair closer to his and pull my t-shirt over my head. As soon as I'm ready, Andy smiles and moves towards me. "You'll have to help me here. You take Olivia, and I'll give you Harry."

"Okay."

As carefully as I can, like I'm almost scared I might break her, I lift Olivia from Andy's chest and move her to mine. Once she's safely moved, Andy lifts Harry and places him alongside his sister, tucks them both back under their blankets, and grins as he admires the scene before him. Olivia stirs a little, unimpressed that she's been removed from one chest onto a slightly harder, hairier one. Harry, on the other hand, seems completely unperplexed.

The pride in Andy's eyes is intense as he looks at me holding our newborns in my arms. "This is all I've ever wanted." He beams, his eyes misting up. I reach for his hand and squeeze it before dragging him towards me. I pull him in and kiss him softly.

"This is perfect," I reply when our lips part, my own eyes a little wet too.

A midwife knocks on the door and comes in to check on everyone and see how we're all getting along. "Aw, would you look at those two." She smiles warmly, looking at our little bundles sleeping on my chest. "It's your turn for cuddles now, is it, Daddy?"

"It is."

She turns to Andy. "And what about you, Dad? You doing okay too?"

He nods. Choked up by it all, his words don't come.

"Aw, bless you, love. It's a miracle, isn't it? Do you have any little outfits to get these two into?"

Andy reaches for the baby bag we brought with us and nods again.

"Well, give yourselves another thirty minutes of cuddling, and then get them dressed. Lucy is all sorted post-birth and settled, and she's looking forward to seeing you all."

"Thank you." I smile at her. Andy has gone back to staring at our twins.

I chuckle. "Will you pull yourself together even for five minutes, man?"

He shakes his head. "I can't. They're too bloody amazing."

"And Daddy Andy thinks I'm the silly one," I whisper across the tops of their heads.

It's early evening by the time all the paperwork is done and Lucy is ready to leave the hospital. The staff have been amazing, going over all the information we already knew but need to be told for the sake of formalities. The babies aren't legally ours until we apply for a parental order. The babies' mum and dad for now will be registered as Paul and Lucy, despite the fact that Andy is biologically their father.

That's just how the law works in the UK because Lucy and Paul are married. We also have to have a special signed permission from Lucy that says we understand all of that, and we have their consent to take the babies home and make decisions on any treatments they might need. Everything is signed and sealed, and it's time for Lucy and the twins to finally leave hospital.

We stand by Lucy's bedside while she looks from one car seat to the other.

"Now, little ones." She smiles at them, tucking them into their seats even more. "It has been an absolute pleasure to be your womb for the last almost nine months, but it's time for us all to go home now. So, you, Miss Olivia, and you, Master Harry, be very good for Daddy Andy and Daddy Chris, and I'm sure they will tell me how you're getting on and send me pictures of you all the time. You are loved so much, you lucky pair." She wipes her eyes and steps towards us. "Take damn good care of those two." She throws her arms around us, and we stand there for a moment, saying our silent goodbyes and thank yous.

"Right." She nods, pulling back from us and reaching for Paul's hand. "Let's go home and see our own kids."

They walk out hand in hand, and we glance at the bed and the two loaded car seats before scooping them up and taking them to the car.

Once Andy has triple-checked everything is secured, we set off for home, back to Drayton, Portsmouth, to introduce Hannah to her new cousins.

Epilogue
Andy

Four years later

Chris has been very shifty about where we're going on our honeymoon. He tells me I'll need my passport, and I was told to tell Fiona there will be a good few weeks of me not being in the office. I have a funny feeling Fi already knows how long I'll be away, and that's a darn sight more than I know right now.

The car has been packed. My mum and Chris's mum have been over to bid us all bon voyage. Now, the kids are all strapped in, and Chris starts the car.

"Are you ready?" he asks, glancing over at me and giving my hand a gentle squeeze.

"As I ever will be with no idea where the hell I'm going!" I fake frown at him. I'm excited. He's been planning this for the best part of six months while I've been planning the wedding, and I know Chris will have planned this out with meticulous precision. "Are you going to tell me where we're going?" I whine.

He laughs and shakes his head. "Not yet." I glare at him and sigh with a smirk.

He's an ass and he knows it, but he's my ass. Mr and Mr Chris Cooper. I glance down at the wedding band on my finger and over at the matching one on his. A glance in the rear-view mirror shows me three cheeky little grins looking back at me.

I shake my head. "Well, come on, then. Let's get to wherever the hell we're going."

***

Morag

The first postcard arrived a few days after they left.

> *Your son is a scheming bugger. I can't believe I'm here in Paris. The kids are bouncing off the walls at the thought of going to Disney, and I'm feeling the same about getting into the Louvre. I bet you were in on this! Bunch of schemers.*
>
> *Much love,*
>
> *Andy, Chris, and the kids xo*

A week later, two postcards arrived on the doorstep at the same time. The first was a special selfie one from Disney. The looks on their faces as they stood in front of the castle with their mouse ears on made me grin. The message on the back was a simple one.

> *We love you. The kids are having a complete*

blast. We've stopped to talk to all the princesses at least three times, and Harry now wants to be Spider-man. It's insane and we're having the best time!

Love, Chris, Andy, Hannah, Olivia, and Harry xox

The second must have been sent the moment they arrived. A photo of the Florence skyline decorated the front.

Oh, Mum. If you had seen the look on Andy's face when we arrived in Florence. I think the penny has dropped and he's sussed what I'm up to. All the artistic places we should have been to in the plans he had for us as youngsters. I can't wait until he realises where we're visiting next.

Love you!

Chris, and Andy, and the kids! xo

Several others followed the first three.

I smile every time one arrives. They called again last night. Andy has finally stopped threatening to kill Chris for being so sneaky, even though he's been secretly enjoying every minute of his honeymoon since they left.

I'm missing them terribly, but it makes my heart full again to see them so happy and finally back together. I'm glad fate decided to give them a little nudge, just like Zoe had attempted. Those boys were meant to be, and I'm very thankful they are finally together.

Also by Drew Duncan

Just Because Series

Because I Need You

Because I Want Him

Because I Didn't Know

Because It's Always You

Serenade Series

Hart Beats

Keep up to date with the latest release - Join Drew's mailing list

About the Author

Drew is an Irish author with a panache for sarcasm and a love of the random, her cynicism knows no bounds, but she's a secret hopeless romantic who likes to let her characters sizzle on the pages.

She lives her with two children, and dreams of escaping to Hampshire, the home of Jane Austen. When she's not writing, you can find her knitting, crocheting, shouting at Ireland playing rugby, and of course reading.

Keep up to date with all the latest releases and info from Drew by joining their mailing list here:
www.drewduncanbooks.co.uk/newsetter